GLASS HOUSE AT JAMESTOWN

GLASS HOUSE AT JAMESTOWN

By Lavinia Dobler

Illustrated by John Jordan

DODD, MEAD & COMPANY / NEW YORK / 1957

The general situation and most of the events described in this book are based upon historical facts. However, certain fictional characters are wholly imaginative; they do not portray and are not intended to portray any actual persons.

Library of Congress Catalog Card Number: 57-8319

Printed in the United States of America
by The Cornwall Press, Inc., Cornwall, N. Y.

To my nephew
Jimmy Finigan
who, like Nat, loves his pets

ACKNOWLEDGMENTS

I wish to thank the following people and organizations:

Lon Dill, Assistant Administrative Director of the Jamestown-Williamsburg-Yorktown National Celebration Commission, for valuable historical data and for his courtesy and hospitality in showing me Jamestown and other historical sites in Virginia.

The Glass Crafts of America, whose booklet, *Glassmaking at Jamestown,* by J. C. Harrington, is the authority for the technical material in my book.

The American Glassware Association, Division H; and the Flint Glass Workers' Union; the joint management-union group, known as the Jamestown Glasshouse Foundation, Inc.; and the National Park Service for building a replica of the original glass house at Jamestown.

Denise Flynn of Harold Farkas Associates, New York City, for important information and historical pictures.

The staff of the American History Room of the Reference Department of the New York Public Library, New York City.

Muriel Fuller, for encouragement and helpful criticism.

Contents

1

Forest Adventure

NAT PECOCK yawned sleepily as he stooped down and searched in the dark for his only pair of boots. Quietly he headed for the door. The cool air of early fall came through the cracks in the high-roofed cabin.

It wasn't yet daybreak and Nat's first thought when he woke had been to roll over and go back to sleep. But nowadays, besides his kitchen duties, Nat had a special job of his own to do. At the thought of it he touched the bag of corn he had carefully hidden in his pocket.

Nat listened, cocking his ear. He thought he could hear a soft call from the pen in the woods that he had built outside the palisaded fort.

The loose slabs of the floor creaked and Nat hesitated. Then he tiptoed to the door, hoping he had not wakened the men sleeping in long rows. Someone moved and Nat looked back. It was young John Laydon, one of the few good carpenters in Virginia. But he did not wake up. Nat silently closed the cabin door and started for the forest.

Nat was the only boy left at Jamestown. Two of the four English boys who had landed in Virginia, May 13, 1607, had perished. The third, Samuel Collier, was with some of the men at the falls of the James River. During the first seventeen months of the colony more than half of the settlers had died from strange diseases. A few had been killed by the Indians.

Thomas Savage, another boy in the colony, had arrived in Jamestown the preceding January on the ship bringing the first supply of provisions. Just the week before, he had been sent to live in Chief Powhatan's village in exchange for an Indian boy, Tomocomo, who was now staying with the colonists.

Nat was disappointed that Thomas was chosen. "I'm as old as he is," the tall boy told his friend, John Laydon. "I'm thirteen, too," he added rebelliously. A shock of yellow hair fell over his forehead. He brushed it back impatiently as he went on. "Why couldn't I have been sent? I want to do something for the colony."

"The council has decided," John said firmly. "It's not merely an honor, but Captain John Smith and the other members believe the way for a lasting peace with the Indians is for us to learn their language and for them to learn ours." He placed a rough hand on Nat's shoulder. His dark eyes and heavy black eyebrows gave his face a determined look. "Maybe this is the way," he continued. "Thomas has a good ear for strange sounds. Already he knows much of the language. Besides, you have duties here."

Nat had had only a glimpse of the new Indian boy, for Tomocomo stayed in the forest most of the time. This morning, as he moved silently into the woods, he realized he had not tried to make friends with Tomocomo. Probably Thomas would have made friends with him by this time. Nat resolved to try and see the boy that very day.

As he pushed through the tangles of oak, pine and sassafras, the early dawn broke through the trees. Nat hurried faster. He was outside the fort now and beyond the palisades made of strong logs. A few more steps and he would be with Mattie.

Mattie was the only thing that was his very own. She had a funny pointed black-and-white face and tiny ears. Her markings—the black patch across her face and around her eyes—made her resemble an owl. When Nat looked at Mattie, he laughed. She was different from any animal he had ever seen in England. Even though she had been his for only a day, having her had eased his disappointment about Thomas and his resentment about kitchen drudgery.

Yesterday, two raccoons had been captured. One had been shot, for raccoon meat was prized as food. Nat had begged hard for the other one. The men had only laughed, but before they could kill it Nat's friend, John Laydon, had intervened.

"Let the boy keep the helpless animal," he said, his voice loud and firm. "Nat hasn't a father or a mother. He should have something he can love and care for. This is a rough life for us, but harder still on the boy."

It was John who offered to help Nat build a pen for the raccoon. "The animal can't sleep in the cabin," he said. "I'll help you build some kind of cage to keep the raccoon safe."

Nat and John had been friends for a long time. Nat remembered that winter day on the London wharf where he hoped to pick up an odd job to earn him a bit of bread. His home and family had been swept away in a recent fire and life had been increasingly hard.

A man's heavy voice startled him as Nat watched the ships that were anchored in the Thames River. "Be ye hungry, lad?"

"Yes, I am, sir," Nat answered truthfully, looking at the man's sturdy build.

"I sail on yon ship with the tide. We're going to Raleigh's land, and found a colony for the king."

"Could I go with you?" Nat's voice was eager.

"Maybe," was the welcome reply. "There are three ships sailing tomorrow—*Susan Constant, Godspeed* and *Discovery*. One hundred men and three boys have signed up. Mayhap you can be the fourth." He offered his warm hand to Nat. "I'm John Laydon."

"Nathaniel Pecock's my name." The boy clasped the stranger's hand. "I'd like to go to a new country."

And so it was that Nat Pecock had sailed on the largest vessel, the *Susan Constant,* December 20, 1606. Five months later they arrived on the peninsula of the James River. But from the very first it had been a disappointment, for Nat was assigned to work in the kitchen. He gathered wood, washed and scoured the pots and pans, and cooked for the hungry, dissatisfied men.

Nat would never forget that he almost didn't get the chance to come to this wonderful new country of Virginia. "It's risky to take boys to America, thousands of miles from England," the officers of the London Company had argued emphatically. But John Laydon, Vicar Robert Hunt and some of the adventurers had finally persuaded the council that young boys were needed.

That day on the wharf John turned to Nat. "If they let you come with us, you'll have to work harder than we do."

"I'm not afraid of hard work," Nat answered. "I want adventure but I'd like to be useful too." Maybe in this new land he would be wanted. Then he wouldn't be alone any more.

Nat hadn't minded the hard work at first because there was so much for everyone to do. But more than a year later he was still in the kitchen and no one offered to take his place or even help.

The settlers talked constantly about gold, but Nat never had the chance to go with the men on these long trips, miles from Jamestown, or on the expedition sent in search of Sir Walter Raleigh's Lost Colony on Roanoke Island. Nat had often wondered what had happened to all those people who had come from England so long ago. After more than twenty years it was still a mystery. He seriously doubted whether the Indians had destroyed the whole settlement. Maybe they had died from disease and hunger.

Nat stopped short on the forest path as he saw Tomocomo standing in front of Mattie's pen. Fear ran through him. Would the Indian boy hurt the raccoon?

Tomocomo laughed softly. Nat had never heard an

Indian laugh before, and at first he thought it was a bird singing in one of the oak trees near the pen.

Tomocomo laughed again, louder. This time it was like water tumbling over rocks. Perhaps he was laughing at the raccoon's playful ways.

"Mattie," Nat called.

The slender boy with shiny bronze skin turned around suddenly and started to run.

"Don't run away," Nat said earnestly.

The Indian boy stopped and looked at him. Nat realized that Tomocomo did not understand English, so he beckoned and then pointed at the raccoon. Tomocomo did not say anything but neither did he run.

"Matoaka wants you," Nat said softly. "Matoaka wants you," he repeated.

Slowly Tomocomo came toward Nat who was now close to the pen. This time the Indian boy seemed to understand. He nodded and smiled.

"Matoaka, Matoaka," Tomocomo said eagerly, pointing at the raccoon.

Nat realized that the Indian boy knew the word *Matoaka.* That was the Indian name of Chief Powhatan's daughter. He had heard the settlers call the Indian princess Pocahontas, but her real name was Matoaka. It meant "playful one." Matoaka was gay, with long black hair and flashing eyes. When the Indians spoke of her, their own eyes sparkled. This girl, who was also thirteen, had been to Jamestown several times to run in the races with the boys. Nat liked Pocahontas and her happy ways and had named his raccoon Matoaka for her.

Nat opened the door of the pen and went in. Mattie ran over to him, her long tail with black rings bobbing up and down. She jumped up and started licking his face.

"Matoaka! You do like me!" He petted her and

Tomocomo laughed again. Nat looked up at the boy who was now peering through the rough wooden slats.

"Come in," Nat called, beckoning to him.

But the Indian boy disappeared silently into the forest.

Nat pulled the bag of corn out of his pocket. Mattie stuck her pointed nose into the leather pouch and started eating the yellow grains.

Presently Nat heard the rustle of leaves. He looked up and there was the Indian boy, holding a fish in his hands.

"Fish?" Nat was puzzled. Would Mattie like that?

"Fish!" Tomocomo repeated in a pleased tone. He came closer.

The raccoon smelled the fish and stopped eating. She reached out and grabbed it from Tomocomo's outstretched hand.

"I didn't know raccoons liked fish," Nat said. "I won't have to feed her corn. I shouldn't take grain from our supplies. They're low, and we don't know when the ship will come."

"Fish, fish, Matoaka," the Indian boy said slowly. He moved closer and began to rub Mattie's nose.

Nat watched them, the Indian boy and the tiny, furry animal he had come to love. This was a way, then, he thought. He, Mattie and Tomocomo would be friends and perhaps he, too, as well as Thomas, would have a real part to play in the Jamestown colony.

2

The New Governor

IN CONTRAST TO NAT, Tomocomo had no special duties. Whenever Nat headed for the forest to gather wood, no matter where the Indian boy was, he suddenly appeared and joined him. These days Nat was seldom lonely because he had Mattie and Tomo.

Tomo had many secrets. He knew where to find roots, grasses, fruits, nuts and gay-colored berries that were good to eat. Nat never knew what to expect as they waded together through high grass, or crawled under thickets of aromatic sassafras or even sat quietly under a tall tree.

Nat found it an exciting game to follow Tomo through the dense forest. He marveled at Tomo's keen eyes. He was fascinated by the way his nose quivered like a rabbit's at sounds and smells.

One day Tomo whispered something to Nat and pointed to a blur in midair. Nat turned but though he tried very hard, all he could see was masses of shining oak leaves and acorns. He heard a zooming sound and looked more closely, hoping to find what Tomo had already seen. At last he spotted a ruby-throated hummingbird. A leaf fluttered. Nat saw a long, thin bill and a tiny body that seemed to be swinging rapidly in the air from side to side as though on a pendulum. Nat looked at Tomo and smiled.

"It's like a large bee," Nat said seriously.

"Me like little bird. Zzzz, zzzzz." Tomo made a humming sound in his throat.

Tomo certainly knew bird calls. He recognized birds by the fluttering sound their wings made as they flew overhead. He seemed to know instinctively where to find the little woodland animals, even though they were concealed under thick brush or were hidden by leaves.

Tomo pointed to a white-faced animal swinging on the branch of a nearby tree. Her babies were in her pouch. Four inquisitive white faces peered down at them. They resembled rats with gray fur. The boys muffled a laugh.

"Apassom," Tomo said.

Nat was excited. He had never before seen a mother animal carry her babies in her pocket. "How did you know where to look?" He was puzzled. Would he too ever have this knowledge?

"Indians have many secrets," Tomo answered quickly. "Apassom like squaw. Wants papoose with her all the time."

It was later the boys learned that the English word for this white-faced animal was opossum.

Nat wished he could walk as noiselessly through the forest as Tomo did, instead of stumbling and often getting scratched by a low-hanging branch. But Tomo wore moccasins of deerskin. If the ship with the second cargo of supplies didn't come soon, Nat, too, would be forced to wear them. He wouldn't mind though. Those soft-leather heeless shoes were comfortable, and they wouldn't be as heavy as his black boots.

When Nat was in the forest he found he could almost forget his fear of fire. Whenever he looked at the huts in the settlement and saw smoke curling from those chimneys that were made of dry straw and mud, his own terrible memories of the London fire came back. Jamestown had had several fires. The big one last January was a nightmare. The flames not only destroyed the church but many of the dwellings, much of the provisions, amunition and even some of the palisades.

After his first horrified cry of "Fire!" Nat had worked until he almost dropped, carrying buckets of water, hoping desperately to save the little church and Vicar Hunt's fine collection of books. But everything burned and nothing was saved.

Vicar Hunt had been proud of his church. When they first landed, Nat and the other colonists had prayed under a sail attached to trees. Then later Vicar Hunt preached in a small building which one of the men called a "homely thing like a barn."

"It's God's house," the minister told Nat and the other settlers. "It has been blessed."

Before the church burned to the ground, Nat used to go often to see his kind friend. Vicar Hunt picked out exciting stories from the big black Book and read out loud to him. The minister was teaching him to read. Nat treasured the *Book of Common Prayer,* one of the few gifts he had ever received. The minister had written in cramped script of the time, *"May you always have faith."*

However, before Captain Christopher Newport, who had arrived in January with the first supply of provisions, sailed back to England, he with the help of the sailors partially rebuilt the church, storehouse, palisades and some of the cabins.

The ship with the second cargo of supplies should have arrived months ago. In the cabins, at the table, at work, all Nat heard was: "When will the ship come?"

"It's long overdue," one man said as he shook his head. "We'll all be dead before we ever see it."

"We might be," John nodded. Everyone was as pessimistic and discouraged as Nat was.

What if the ship never came? What if those vital food supplies were lost in the Atlantic or were taken by pirates or Spaniards? Nat dreaded another starving time. There were so many things that could happen to a ship. It was a long distance from London to Jamestown. Nat had been tossed about in the *Susan Constant* for five weary months.

The colonists were busier now than they had been for some time. There was a reason, and Nat was well aware of it. Captain John Smith, who had just been elected president of the council, was determined to change the lazy ways of the settlers. The men clearly showed by their actions that they resented one-man control instead of rule by council.

The governor was a military man. Nat admired his soldierly manner, the way he proudly walked and marched. He wore his broad-brimmed Jacobean hat on his red hair with an air of assurance. Like the other men, he wore his hat constantly, even when he was working in his cabin. Nat had heard Captain Smith complain bitterly that first year about the poorly constructed three-sided fort. All the houses in the Jamestown fort were poorly built.

"Jamestown would have less trouble with the Indians," he said many times, "and we certainly would be more secure if we had a larger fort." But since Captain Smith was not then the leader and not popular with the settlers, Governor Wingfield and the members of the council ignored his complaints. It had been like that from the beginning.

Nat remembered how wonderful it had seemed, after long months of being tossed about in the small ship, at last to sight land. On April 26th they had stopped at Cape Henry and put up a cross in gratitude for their safe passage. More than a fortnight later, on May 13, 1607, they sailed up the James River, named then and there for their king, and moored their ships under flowering white dogwood and pink Judas trees.

But Captain Smith was in the hold in irons. He was a prisoner under suspicion of mutiny. Irons or not, he boasted that the London Company had, with King James's approval, named him a member of the council for the new colony, and all would be well when the strong box was unlocked. The London Company had given strict instructions to Captain Newport, admiral of the three little ships, that the iron box was not to be opened until the venturers arrived in Virginia. On April 26th at Cape Henry they unlocked the box. Names of the seven members of the council were sealed inside this box.

Trouble started immediately after it was opened. The men were furious that Captain Smith was on the governing board, and the other six councilmen refused to seat him. They all voiced strong grievances against the young soldier with the red beard.

"Smith has an irritating way of telling people how to

do things better," John said to Vicar Hunt in Nat's hearing.

"Maybe Captain Smith can perform these tasks better than others," Vicar Hunt said slowly, looking directly at John. "He is not a quitter. Even though he is irritating, you will find in the long run that he's right. I think he understands better than anyone else the problems and struggles this society will have," he added.

Nat never ceased to appreciate Vicar Hunt's kind consideration for others. He heard Captain Smith once say of the Anglican clergyman: "At sea and on land, he is our peacemaker. Many times he has quenched the flames of envy and dissension with the water of patience." Nat was glad that Captain Smith admired Vicar Hunt in the same way he did.

Most of the venturers were satisfied when Wingfield was elected the first president of the council. Not so Captain Smith. He had been allowed to work but, still smarting at his imprisonment, he criticized the governor to everyone who would listen. "Wingfield has made a serious blunder in not having military drill," Captain Smith sputtered. "These men need discipline. Does he call this a fort? All we have is boughs of trees!"

The men had to admit there was no one in the settlement who had seen as many fortified places as Captain Smith had. On board ship Nat had listened eagerly as he told about his travels through Turkey and other countries in eastern Europe where they had log forts. This kind could be reproduced in stoneless, tidewater Virginia.

No one at Jamestown was more pleased than Captain Smith when the council admitted him a month after they landed. Vicar Hunt had interceded for him. "They've accepted him only because of his knowledge of wooden forts," John told Nat.

"Isn't that a good reason?" Nat asked.

"I'm afraid it means trouble," was John's reply.

Unfortunately most of the work on the fort was finished by this time, so Captain Smith could not make too many changes. Nat had seen the stone Tower of London so he didn't think this wooden fort was very strong. It was triangular in shape with a bulwark at each of the three corners. Three bulwarks—solid, wall-like structures—were shaped like big half-moons.

The men struggled as they unloaded the heavy ordnance from the ships. Nat watched them bring the artillery from the river bank. "I'd like to help," he said.

"We need strong, sturdy men, not boys," one of the workers said gruffly. "Why strain your back when you don't have to?"

After the cannon were in the bulwarks, Nat lifted one of the black balls. "It's heavy," Nat said, holding it with both his hands.

"Sure it is, but heavier balls will kill more Indians," the guard answered.

But now, more than a year and a half later, the fort was being enlarged from a three-sided to a five-sided enclosure. This was Captain Smith's first important achievement as president of the council. Nat watched every change that was made. The space inside the fort, which was only about an acre, was almost doubled and the settlers could now build more houses, if they could find men who had the time and inclination to construct them.

The governor tightened up the watch. He trained each of the units so that a competent military guard was on duty at all times.

Nat kept hoping Captain Smith would order him to train with the rest of the men. But he didn't.

"I wish I could trade places with you," John said. "I

detest a soldier's duties, and I certainly don't like standing guard."

"I'd like to be a soldier and help protect Jamestown," Nat answered. "I wouldn't give Captain Smith any trouble," he said earnestly, "as some of the men do."

"The governor rules Jamestown with an iron hand," John said bitterly. "Just wait until Captain Newport returns with the second supply! Then Citizen Smith will have to obey another captain's orders!"

The settlers resented the hard work of leveling off the drill field to the west. They called it Smithfield. When the Indians came every Saturday to watch, the men were even more indignant. Sometimes Nat counted as many as a hundred Indians. He guessed they wanted to see how a file of English musketeers could batter a mark set up on a tree.

Nat watched enviously the activity on the waterfront. Captain Smith had given instructions that the small boats were to be put in shape for an important trading expedition.

He knew as well as the governor did that food supplies were low. If they couldn't get provisions from the Indians, there would certainly be a starving time and more men would get sick and die. Last spring they had not plowed enough land or planted many seeds. The harvest this fall was meager. Their only hope was to barter with the Indians for maize, or Indian corn, and they got boats ready to go upriver for this.

Nat was surprised when Governor Smith announced that Lieutenant George Percy would head the trading expedition. Many times Nat had heard Percy sneeringly call Captain Smith the "vaine glorious" governor. He was a long-faced man with an enormous nose and a sour look.

He was also the brother of the powerful Earl of Northumberland.

Nat went down to the river and watched enviously as the boats sailed out of sight. They were headed for Chesapeake Bay. He wished he were sailing northward, too, with a chance at adventure and not routine kitchen chores.

3

"A Bird Comes Sailing"

BECAUSE OF Governor Smith's strict discipline Nat didn't dare go into the forest now as often as he wanted to. When he did go it was to gather wood for the kitchen fires. That was one of his chores. "Master Woodgatherer," he muttered rebelliously. "That's what I am."

It was at these times Nat especially missed Thomas Savage, for Tomo refused to help him. When Thomas was there, they both used to gather wood.

"Squaw work." Tomo shrugged his shoulders. His manner was almost haughty. "Not for brave Indian."

"But there aren't any women here, Tomo," Nat tried to explain. "We need wood for the fires. Someone has to do it. It happens to be my job but I don't like it."

Nat thought Tomo surely understood the reason he had this chore, but that didn't make any difference. Tomo still wouldn't help. The Indian boy would disappear into the woods, making Nat more indignant than ever. Nat resentfully gathered fallen branches and dragged tree limbs toward the settlement.

It always seemed to Nat that just when he was almost in sight of the fort and most of the heavy work was over, Tomo appeared, smiling and chewing on some juicy grass or root. When Tomo offered him some, Nat wanted very much to say "No," but he was always curious to find out what it tasted like.

Nat couldn't get angry at Tomo. He was much too grateful for all the forest surprises that Tomo shared with him.

But that didn't stop Nat from wishing Tomo would help him. How could he figure out a way to make him? He didn't believe it was because Tomo felt superior, although sometimes Nat felt that way. Maybe if he didn't resent his work so much he wouldn't be hurt by Tomo's attitude.

There were other grievances too. Why didn't Captain Smith let him hunt instead of gather firewood? There was dignity to that. But the governor was firm. "Firearms are for the men," he said sternly.

One day Nat was struggling unusually hard with two big tree limbs. He stopped for a moment when he came to the clearing in sight of the fort, and leaned against a tree to rest. As he wiped the perspiration from his forehead, Tomo appeared.

"Good day!" he called cheerfully.

Nat looked up. Tomo had a wild turkey flung over his bare shoulder.

"How did you get it?" Nat asked, a trifle enviously.

"Easy," Tomo said casually.

The tall boy held up a bow and arrow which he had hidden behind him.

"A bow and arrow!" Nat said, reaching for it. He touched the bow. It was made from thin green wood and rawhide.

"Bow and arrow?" Tomo repeated. "Want it?"

Nat nodded as he tested the limber bow. Then he aimed. "Why didn't I think of this before?" he asked. "Guess I had my heart set on a gun."

"Bow and arrow much better than bad gun," Tomo said. "Gun makes Indian have fear," he shook his head. "Indian afraid when white man uses gun. Loud noise hurts. . ." Then Tomo paused, covering his ears with his hands.

"Ears," Nat filled in the missing word.

Tomo pulled on the lobe of his right ear. "Ears?" he looked puzzled. "Not ears like corn?"

Nat laughed. He had never thought that the word had two meanings. There really was no connection between them. Tomo was making him more aware of his own language.

"We're friends," Nat said. "I wouldn't shoot at you. But I still want a gun."

"Two boys friends," Tomo said. He held up two brown fingers.

"Yes, we're friends, but why don't you help me?" Nat asked. "Good friends help each other."

The Indian boy shook his head. "Squaw work." He

shrugged his shoulders and disappeared behind some oaks. A few minutes later he reappeared, waving a leather thong. "Maybe this help you?"

"Where did you get it?" Nat was curious. He knew Tomo hadn't had time to go back to the cabin and return.

"Tomocomo has secrets," he half smiled.

The Indian boy helped tie the leather thong securely around the tree branches. Then he stood and watched Nat pull the heavy load. Finally he went over and pulled too.

When they reached the door of the cabin, Tomo said, "Reason Indian brave won't do this—work much too hard."

Nat nodded. He regretted that he couldn't be with Tomo more of the time. If Tomo would only help him in the kitchen he could be. He said as much.

"Me not squaw," the Indian boy said shaking his head vigorously. "Brave Indian."

"I'm not a squaw either. I'm a brave Englishman, but I have to work in the kitchen," Nat answered a little defiantly.

"For you, not for me," Tomo answered and started for the forest.

Nat wished he didn't feel the way he did about the endless work in the kitchen. Tomo's attitude made him more resentful and dissatisfied.

Somehow Nat had the feeling that things might be different when the big ship arrived. But as the leaves turned golden and dropped from the trees and the days became steadily colder, Nat lost hope. Maybe the ship had been attacked by pirates, or perhaps a storn had torn it to pieces.

Nat could not discuss his fears with Tomo. The Indian boy said he had paddled a canoe on the bay when it was like shining glass. Nat doubted whether he had ever paddled as far as the ocean, and of course he had never seen a big ship.

Even John Laydon became more silent about the ship from England. John's fears were just as real as Nat's but John seemed to have more faith.

"Any day now that ship will sail gloriously into the bay and up the James River to our peninsula," John said.

Nat hoped John was right. He would sometimes steal a few hours from the kitchen and run as fast as he could to the river, looking for the overdue ship. Tomo generally was with him. There never was much time to fret, though, because there were fish to catch for Mattie and the men. He wished the men liked fish as much as the raccoon did.

Tomo and Nat recently had found a clay pit. They scooped up some in a wooden bucket and Nat tried to make a clay animal to resemble Mattie.

When the kitchen work was done, Nat hurried to the river bank so that he would be near water as he shaped the clay.

This morning Tomo was nowhere to be found, so Nat had gone to the river's edge alone.

"Boy." Nat quickly turned around. This was occasionally Tomo's name for him.

"Where have you been?" he asked.

"In the pit." Tomo held up a handful of mud. "More clay for Matoaka."

Tomo's interest in the clay animal pleased Nat, for it encouraged him to keep working.

"Make good Matoaka," Tomo said.

But Nat couldn't get the long, narrow nose shaped like the raccoon's.

"It doesn't look like Mattie," Nat said discouragedly.

"Try again," Tomo urged.

So Nat tried again. He kneaded the new lump of clay, pounded it flat to get the air bubbles out and formed the clay into a square. Over and over again he tried to shape it to look like a reclining raccoon. Nat was so engrossed in his efforts that nothing else seemed quite so important.

Suddenly Tomo called out. "Bird, big bird!" He jumped up and disappeared in the underbrush.

In the distance Nat saw a black object on the water. "The ship! The ship has come! It has come at last!" Nat jumped up, the clay falling out of his lap and onto the ground. He waved excitedly.

He looked around for Tomo. He must not be afraid of the wonderful ship. Nat ran into the woods calling to his friend, "The ship is here!"

He stopped and stood among the trees that blazed with gold and red. It was too bad that Tomo was afraid of the ship when everyone else in the colony longed for its coming. Tomo was afraid because he had never seen a big ship before, Nat realized. What could he tell the Indian boy so that he would understand? Then he thought of their pet.

"Mattie is good," Nat said loudly to the trees. "The ship is good." He paused, hoping Tomo would come from his hiding place. "The ship will not harm you. The ship is good."

Nearby bushes rustled. Tomo stuck his head out. "A bird comes sailing?" Tomo asked. "It is good?"

"Very good," Nat nodded. "It's the best news we could

ever have." He smiled. "Let's be the first to tell John and Governor Smith."

"A bird comes sailing," Tomo smiled, too.

They raced to the fort, the clay animal forgotten.

4
The Glassmakers Arrive

As NEWS OF the ship's arrival spread through the settlement this October morning in 1608, Nat watched the men run out of the cabins with the pointed roofs. Even the guards on duty left their posts and hurried to the river.

"The ship's here!" they shouted. "It's come at last!" Nat had never seen the colonists so excited. It was like a celebration. The sky was a deeper sapphire and the leaves seemed more golden than they had an hour before.

"I knew the ship would come. I think it is the *Mary Margaret,*" Nat told Tomo excitedly. "Vicar Hunt promised us that our prayers would be answered."

How he wished the minister could have lived long enough to see the colony so joyful. More than anyone else in Jamestown, Vicar Hunt had steadfastly believed that the ship would come. The chaplain had died last summer and there had been less praying since. There was no one now to administer communion. Nat felt that if the settlers could have had the faith the minister had shown, there would be less dissension and jealousy. Maybe this ship would bring another vicar to take his place.

Vicar Hunt would not have liked Nat's impatient attitude. Nat almost heard his kind voice. "Be patient, my boy," he had said to him many times. "The best things in life do not happen overnight. Your opportunity to help Jamestown will come."

Nat looked out over the broad river and saw several smaller boats. They were not large enough to have crossed the rough ocean. These were the boats belonging to the Indian trading expedition headed by George Percy. He must have met the big ship and decided to return. Nat wondered what Captain Smith would say about this. Lieutenant Percy evidently had made his own decision. Captain Smith's orders to him had been to get food for the winter. If the ship from England brought adequate provisions, then maybe he would not mind that Percy had disobeyed him. But Nat knew the governor did not like his orders disregarded.

As the ship slowly approached, Tomo moved closer to Nat. The Indian boy was afraid. Nat could feel him trembling.

"A bird comes sailing?" Tomo asked. Then he repeated it: "A bird comes sailing?"

"It's a ship," Nat explained, "larger than any bird. It has square white sails instead of wings." Nat could understand why Tomo called the ship a bird. He had watched sea gulls floating on the water and in the distance the ship looked as if it were a bird sailing.

"Where did the bird come from?" Tomo asked.

"From far across the ocean, from England where I used to live," Nat answered.

"England?" Tomo asked. "Would I like England?"

"Not as well as your own country," Nat answered. "There are many people living there, more than all the Indians belonging to the Powhatan federation. I lived in a big place, London, where there are large buildings and not many trees or flowers."

"That is bad." Tomo shook his head. "Are there many birds?"

"You mean ships like this one?" Nat asked.

Tomo nodded.

"Yes, on London's big river, the Thames, there are many ships," Nat answered. "This one is three-masted. The ship I sailed on, the *Susan Constant,* also had three long masts or poles. It carried square sails and flew the red and blue flag of England just like the one that waves over the fort at Jamestown."

As the ship moved in closer to the river bank, the colonists became more excited than ever. Finally it was moored to trees in six fathoms of water.

John Laydon and others had joined Tomo and Nat.

"I wonder what kind of supplies the ship has brought this time?" a man standing near the boys asked.

"Whatever they brought we'll welcome," John answered. "We need provisions—everything."

"No one will argue that point," another said.

As the *Mary Margaret* dropped anchor, the trumpets played loudly. Captain Newport was in the bow waiting to come ashore. He was richly dressed and his medals shone brilliantly in the sun. His cape was lined with red and his padded breeches were made of velvet. His broad-brimmed hat sat at a jaunty angle on his head. His boots with wide cuffs had large metal buckles that sparkled as he walked. Nat looked from the captain down at his own worn-out doublet and breeches. He felt guilty that his shoes were so old. The London Company had advised each emigrant to provide himself with four pairs of shoes, but Nat had no money, so he had come to the new country with only one pair. That was sixteen months ago!

"There's the captain who was in command of the ship," Nat said to Tomo with a trace of pride in his voice.

"Captain Newport is a good mariner. He knows the seas," John said. "Of course the ship came through."

The crowd parted for Governor Smith. As president of the council, he was the first to greet Captain Newport. The latter swaggered off the ship, followed slowly by about seventy people, including a pretty young girl and an older woman.

At the sight of the women cheers rang out. To the colonists they were the most interesting passengers on board. The rather plump matron was wearing a purple gown with a lace ruff at the neck.

There was a stir in the crowd. A man was struggling to get through. It was Master Forrest. "My wife, my wife!" he cried. "At last she's come!"

Mistress Forrest was as happy as her husband.

Nat was fascinated by the younger woman for he had almost forgotten how lovely one could be. She wore a plain gray dress of linsey-woolsey with a long graceful skirt. Her light hair was held in place by a tight-fitting cap. As she looked up at the fifty men who swarmed as close as they dared to the river bank, she hesitated. When several eager swains waded into the river, she seemed embarrassed. Their boots quickly filled with water and they scrambled out on the bank again.

Nat could understand how the girl felt. He had never liked too much attention. It almost made him afraid. But Nat sympathized, too, with the men. No wonder they were staring. They hadn't seen a white woman for more than a year and a half! Indeed, these were the first two white women to come to Jamestown!

John Laydon hurried to assist the girl to the river bank. She looked up at John and smiled.

"You lucky dog," one man shouted.

"That isn't fair," another yelled. "He has won her already. The rest of us haven't a chance!"

"You're not as good-looking as John is," another said as the rest laughed loudly.

"Ann, Ann Burras, wait for me!" Mistress Forrest called. The girl nodded. She seemed shy and winsome. Nat hoped the men's actions had not frightened her.

How pleasant to have women in the settlement, Nat thought. Perhaps Ann and Mistress Forrest would help with the cooking. Then the food would certainly taste better.

It took quite some time for the passengers to get off the *Mary Margaret.* Nat noticed a group of men carrying heavy bags who stayed close together. They were stocky, with fair hair and ruddy complextions. As Nat came nearer he heard them talking. The language wasn't English and it wasn't Indian.

A man with straight flaxen hair looked at Nat and smiled. *"Guten Tag,"* he said.

It sounded like a friendly greeting. "Hello," Nat called back, returning the smile.

Nat edged closer to Captain Newport and Governor Smith.

"We've brought eight Poles and Germans over to make glass," Nat heard Captain Newport say to Governor Smith. "They're craftsmen and we're fortunate having them."

"Glass, you say?" Governor Smith seemed surprised.

"That's a thriving business," Captain Newport answered quickly. "It should do well in Jamestown, since Virginia has the right kind of sand. We haven't found gold yet, unfortunately, and the London Company has to make this settlement pay. But England can't be dependent indefinitely on the glassmakers in Italy. With the knowledge that these Germans and Poles have, there's no reason why glassmaking can't become a profitable industry here. We'll start building the glass house at once."

"But the men here have no interest in this kind of work," Governor Smith tried to explain.

"They can learn," Captain Newport said, his voice firm. "England has to import too many things. Glass is in greater demand each year. England must have her own industries and there is no reason why her colonies can't supply materials and men." There was a note of finality in Captain Newport's voice.

So this was a command! At least it sounded that way to Nat.

"We're here to find gold, not to make glass," a disgruntled man with a black beard said who was standing near Nat. The boy recognized him as one of the many adventurers who had come to Virginia to seek his fortune. He scowled as he rubbed his bushy black eyebrows.

"We're not laborers, we're gentlemen," another added as he waved his plumed hat. "The Spaniards found gold in the New World. Why can't we?"

"Gold! Gold!" several men chorused.

Nat couldn't visualize these men making glass. He had a vague idea that you had to work in front of a blazing fire in order to melt the sand and other materials. Probably it wasn't too pleasant work for lazy men.

If most of the settlers intended to take this attitude, what would happen? But they weren't their own master. The London Company was. That company was determined to make money from the colony in America. When the *Mary Margaret* sailed back, would some of them return to England? Nat doubted it. Most of the men were still confident they'd find gold.

In that one determination they were united. Actually, there had been few gold expeditions, and Nat wasn't certain they knew how to find the ore, unless it was right under their noses or sticking out of a ledge of rock. He guessed that lumps of gold were picked up like bright stones or rocks. So far he hadn't had the chance to go on an expedition. But he hoped to sometime.

The men were gamblers. They had left England because there they couldn't find what they wanted. A new, unexplored country appealed to them. Nat doubted whether most of them had wives and children in England. Otherwise they would not have come to such a faraway land. Master Forrest was an exception. He had often talked about his wife, and had planned for her to come to Virginia ever since he had arrived. Nat was certain Master Forrest would now want to make Jamestown his home for the rest of his life.

Even on this great day the men were dissatisfied. Nat was conscious of discontented murmers from the settlers around him. The word had spread quickly about the new industry.

"I'd like to help build that glass house," John Laydon said. There was an eagerness in his voice. John had helped build many of the high-roofed cabins and the little church.

Nat knew, though, how disappointed Governor Smith was that so many of the men's only interest was to hunt for gold. Jamestown needed men who were willing to work hard at farming, at making clapboard and at other things that would build a permanent settlement.

Glassmaking sounded different to Nat. He remembered seeing all kinds of bright glass in fascinating shapes in the shops of London. Glassmakers who had beauty in their hearts must have made this glass.

If the two captains couldn't persuade the men to work in the glass house, what would happen? He'd be willing to do anything if only he didn't have those kitchen chores! But who could help him? The glassmakers?

"Maybe I have a chance," Nat whispered to Tomo. "Maybe I can work in the glass house. I'm going to try."

Tomo nodded, but Nat knew that the Indian boy could not possibly realize what it could mean to him. A bird flew overhead. Suddenly Nat thought of his clay model of the raccoon. Where was it? He couldn't remember.

"Tomo," Nat said, "my clay Mattie. Let's find it."

The Indian boy nodded.

5

Orders from London

NAT AND TOMO turned to weave their way through the crowd. Suddenly Nat heard Governor Smith call out in a loud voice: "Captain Newport has an announcement from the London Council."

Nat turned to Tomo. "We can't leave now. This may be important to us."

The old and new settlers formed a half-circle around the two captains and waited.

Captain Newport unrolled a large parchment scroll. He studied the group. "I have serious business to report," he said. "The London Company has already lost considerable money on this venture in Virginia." He shook his head. "When I sailed from England in the spring, I was given definite instructions which must be followed. I shall read them." He adjusted a pair of tiny spectacles on the bridge of his long nose.

In a clear voice, Captain Newport read: " 'The London Company urges the council to spend more time in the preparation of marketable products, such as glass, frankincense and clapboard.' " The captain looked up from the parchment as a brisk wind rustled the document. "We brought some glassmakers with us on the *Mary Margaret*. They are expert craftsmen and they know their skills. We will start immediately to build the glass house. We expect to make some glass articles this fall. In fact, I have instructions to bring back to London samples of glass made in Jamestown."

The parchment reminded Nat of the long sheet of instructions the London Company had given Captain Newport almost two years before when the three ships had first set out for the new country. They had a hard time deciding on the place to settle because of the conditions set down by the council. Nat had memorized these requirements. As he recalled them now, he thought again how difficult they were.

> The settlement was to be a hundred miles up some river so as to be free of attack from the sea.
>
> It must not be inhabited by savages.
>
> It must be so placed that a bark of fifty tons could lay provisions ashore with ease.
>
> The settlement must also be easy to defend, set in a spot free from swamp fever.
>
> Natives should not be allowed to settle between it and the sea.

Cape Henry, Point Comfort, even Archer's Hope Creek had either not been far enough up the river, or the Indians lived too close or a boat could not get near enough to the shore to unload easily.

"Clapboard sells for a good price," Captain Newport went on. Nat knew that clapboard was used for paneling rooms in a house. "We will ship back a large supply this time. The company is well aware of the dense forests around Jamestown. That is one reason why they've decided on the glass industry. We'll need a goodly number of men to chop the wood and prepare the clapboard for shipment, collect the frankincense or resin, as well as to work in the glass house."

The men began to mutter rebelliously. Some of them shook their heads. They did not want to work as laborers in a glass house or in the woods.

Nat hoped Captain Newport wouldn't say anything more about glassmaking or wood chopping. The men would endure only so much. A tiny spark could start a rebellion. In times past they had been on the verge of refusing to obey. Since Captain Smith had been elected president, there had been some order. The men now knew who was in command. Except that Captain Newport, as the direct representative from the London Company, had more power than Governor Smith. Perhaps Captain Newport would be more lenient. But if he meant what he said he would demand even more of the men than the governor did.

"However, glass and clapboard isn't the whole story," Captain Newport said, smiling. "The London Company has given instructions that gold be sought more actively."

"Hooray!" the men shouted. Some even threw their large black hats in the air and nimbly caught them before they fell to the ground.

"If we find gold," Captain Newport went on, removing his spectacles and holding them in his hand, "our fortunes will be made and we'll never have to worry about money.

Neither will the London Company. The success of this Jamestown venture is then assured!"

"If we could only find it," John said, turning to Nat and Tomo. "But I disagree with Captain Newport. The success of this colony does not depend entirely on whether we find gold."

Before Nat could answer, Captain Newport continued: "The London Company has also given instructions for the colonists to search diligently for the Roanoke settlers of Sir Walter Raleigh's Lost Colony."

The captain paused. "It's a great mystery how that colony on Roanoke Island disappeared. No one has had any word for over twenty years!" He paused. "We can't believe that the Indians destroyed the people and the settlement. We earnestly pray that they are still alive. We know other Englishmen have searched for the Lost Colony, including John White, but if we could find those brave people, we would be honored by King James and all of England. As you know, the records and maps show that the Roanoke settlement isn't too far from here."

"Maybe there's gold there too," one adventurer spoke up.

Captain Newport nodded. "There could be." He looked down at the document in his hand. "The London officials recognize the importance of keeping on good terms with Chief Powhatan. We will present him with a crown and gifts at an impressive ceremony."

"What will the chief do with a crown?" one man asked with a shout of laughter.

"What does a crown mean to an Indian?" another agreed.

"As Englishmen, subjects of His Majesty, King James the First," Captain Newport insisted, "the greatest honor we can bestow on Powhatan, chief of the powerful Indian federation, is a gold crown."

"Maybe we all don't agree a crown is that great an honor," a third said.

"We are subjects of the Crown of England," Captain Newport said sternly.

"Long live the king!" several yelled.

"Long live King Powhatan!" others cried out.

But the idea still seemed funny to the men.

"I wish we were playing with Mattie," Nat whispered.

"Me, too," Tomo nodded.

They edged their way through the crowd as quickly as they could. As they passed by the Poles and Germans, Nat said to them, "I'm glad you've come to this new country." His voice was sincere.

One of the men smiled. *"Danke schön"* he said. He had a kind face, Nat thought. Maybe he liked boys and would help them.

Tomo and Nat gathered berries growing by the river bank to give to the raccoon. They found the bucket of clay as well as the model which fortunately was not broken.

"I'll have to study Mattie more closely before I go on with this," Nat said, looking at his unfinished work.

"Bring Matoaka here," Tomo suggested. "She likes water. She catch fish. We watch her."

"Can raccoons catch fish?" Nat asked.

Tomo nodded.

"But she might run away."

"No, not with this." Tomo produced a rawhide thong.

"That's an idea," Nat said with interest. "Maybe we can make a collar for her and tie the rawhide to that."

"We are three friends," Tomo smiled. "We want to be together."

6

A Surprise

THE RACCOON had been sleeping under her favorite oak. As the boys approached her pen she pricked up her tiny ears.

"Mattie, where are you?" Nat greeted her cheerfully.

She stretched her legs and then raced excitedly from one end of the pen to the other, climbing up on the wooden slats.

"Matoaka have good day?" the Indian boy asked. The raccoon squealed happily.

Tomo always called the raccoon by her Indian name. Nat guessed it was easier for him to say Matoaka than Mattie. He liked the soft notes in Tomo's voice when he slowly spoke English or his own tongue. It reminded Nat of small bells tinkling.

Today, when the boys unlocked the door, the raccoon jumped up on Nat and licked his face with her rough red tongue. Then she raced over to Tomo and greeted him in the same joyful way.

"Mattie likes us," Nat said, rubbing the raccoon's ears and pointed nose. "She has two masters."

Tomo nodded. He was busy with the deerskin thong. When the boys tried to place the strap around her neck, Mattie looked hurt and crouched low to the ground.

"Mattie, we want to take you to the river," Nat explained patiently. "We won't make this too tight, and it won't hurt you."

"Fish, water," Tomo pleaded. But the raccoon seemed frightened. Her ears drooped and she dragged her body on the dry oak leaves.

"She's afraid." Nat patted her furry gray-and-black body. "Mattie doesn't understand what we want to do."

"Hold her," Tomo suggested.

Since she wasn't much bigger than a large cat, Nat picked her up gently and the raccoon snuggled in his arms, hiding her face in his long full sleeve. "Guess she feels safe now," Nat said.

As they walked through the woods, Nat talked to her as if she were human, telling her about the big ship and the new settlers who had just come to Virginia.

"Mattie, I think the two pretty ladies and the men who speak a different language will like you too." Nat scratched her ear that quivered.

Mattie looked up at him and cocked her ears. Nat laughed. She had such a funny expression with those black patches that outlined her eyes. "Sometimes you make me think of a pirate," Nat said as he rubbed her more roughly.

Tomo had run on ahead toward the bank of the James River. When Nat and the raccoon came out of the forest, the Indian boy was waiting for them with his hands behind him. Nat guessed he had a surprise. When Mattie smelled the fish, she leaped out of Nat's arms and ran to Tomo. She sniffed excitedly and then grabbed the pike from him.

Grasping the fish tightly in her mouth, the raccoon looked up and down the river bank and then waded into the water. In a few minutes she started to wash the fish, holding it firmly with her front paws.

Nat burst out laughing. "Isn't she funny?" She had so many unexpected tricks that he was constantly amused by what she did.

"Matoaka likes clean food," Tomo said seriously. "She likes it moist."

"Did you know she would do this?" Nat asked.

Tomo's black head bobbed. "When raccoons are near clean water they wash their food. I have watched them many times." It was a long explanation for Tomo. Nat was amazed how quickly he was learning to speak English. His interest in Mattie had undoubtedly taught the Indian boy many new words.

"We must get her a larger bowl and be more careful that she always has fresh water in her pen," Nat said.

"I will make bowl from wood," Tomo suggested. "You make Matoaka out of clay. I will find big log and burn out the inside."

"That's a wonderful idea," Nat agreed.

Since the strap was long, the raccoon was free to wander a short distance along the river bank. Suddenly they heard a splash and Mattie came out of the water with a fish in her mouth.

"She is quick," Tomo said. "Matoaka catches fish the way I do." He was pleased.

"I didn't believe you when you said raccoons could catch fish," Nat said.

Still holding the fish in her mouth, Mattie looked around. She walked over to a shallow pool of water and proceeded to wash it.

"But it's already clean, Mattie," Nat said, more amazed than ever. "You just brought it out of the river."

"That is the way they do when they are near water," Tomo said knowingly.

As Mattie ate the food she had caught, Nat patiently molded the clay. "I wish I could show Mattie eating that fish," he said.

"Too hard," Tomo shook his head.

Nat agreed. "I've never tried to make an animal out of clay before. It's so much harder than rolling out a ball or making something square."

"Try many, many times," Tomo said.

Nat never ceased to marvel at Tomo's calm attitude. Nat wanted to get things done as quickly as possible but time seemed to mean nothing to Tomo.

"I need someone to help me," Nat sighed. "John can't and neither can anyone else that I can think of. The men would laugh if they saw me playing with clay." Then he looked up at Tomo. "I have an idea. If those men who speak a different language are glassmakers, they must know a lot about clay. Maybe they could tell me what's wrong."

He glanced at the sky. The sun was low in the west.

"I have to get back to the kitchen. It's late!" He put the model in the wooden bucket and started running toward the fort. "You stay here with Mattie for a while and then take her back to her pen. Don't forget the clay I'm working on!"

7

Glass House

WHEN NAT RETURNED to the settlement, he saw small groups standing in the square. The men were arguing loudly. The adventurers were still disturbed at the report from the London Company. Their voices rose above the rustle of the oak leaves and the moaning of the restless wind.

Nat noticed one man who seemed especially angered. He shook his fist at the Germans and Poles who were in front of one of the cabins. Was it possible some of the old settlers blamed the glassmakers for these new problems that faced them? Nat felt sorry for the foreigners who had recently left their homes in Europe for an uncertain future in an undeveloped country. Even if they didn't understand English, Nat was certain they knew by the men's rude actions and harsh voices that they were being blamed.

With a sad shake of his head one of the foreigners turned his back on the Englishmen. Nat recognized him as the man with yellow hair and reddish face he had spoken to that morning. The stranger had smiled back at him and had said something in his own language. Nat wondered what his name was.

He looked around the market place, hoping to see Mistress Forrest and the girl. They must be in their own house. He hoped so, because the language some of the men were using was not fit for anyone's ears—certainly not for genteel ladies. Nat knew the men in the colony had become careless in their talk. Even he had cringed at times when he had to listen. Since two women had come to Jamestown, he hoped the men would be more careful.

Right now Nat was troubled about these men who had been in the colony as long as he had. He wished they were a different type. Then they would welcome this chance the London Company was giving them to learn a trade. The settlement needed men who would work hard, prepare the ground, plant seed so that there would be food for the lean months. With glass and clapboard to get ready there would be no time to work in the fields. Nat shuddered at the thought of another starving period.

He was curious to hear more of what the dissatisfied men were saying, but he didn't dare stay. There were vegetables to peel and meat to roast. He headed toward the big kitchen. Sometimes he dreaded his chores as much as the venturers dreaded work.

At least he wouldn't have to worry about Mattie. Tomo would take the raccoon back to her pen, feed her and play with her until the gong sounded for supper. That gong. What a contrast to the Bow bells of London! He missed their friendliness. After his family died, the bells had consoled him with their beautiful chime. Every time the dinner gong sounded here it seemed to say "Duty, Nat duty."

When Nat opened the door of the big cabin he saw to his amazement a group of men in the dining room. Spread out on the hand-hewn table in front of them lay large parchment sheets. They must be maps and plans, Nat decided.

"Captain Newport has already reported to the company that this country has an abundant supply of wood," he heard one of the men say, looking at some kind of document.

"We can't deny that," another answered quickly. "We are surrounded by forests–oak, pine, black walnut, ash, elm, cypress, white poplar and cedar."

"That's why the officials decided glass and clapboard were good products for Virginia."

Nat recognized the deep voice of John Laydon.

"Glassmaking requires a goodly supply of water, so the report suggests that the glass house be built near the river," John added.

"In that case the building can be close to the fort," another spoke up. "Transportation is easy and then there won't be the fear of being attacked by the Indians."

"Most of the ground around the fort has already been cleared," John said. "Wheat and other vegetables which are necessary to our existence are growing." He looked directly at the men. "Those furnaces will burn many cords of wood. This glass house must be in a densely wooded area, away from the settlement, even though the foreigners will be vulnerable to the Indians. The report says there will be four furnaces."

Nat didn't want to hear any more. The glass house with four furnaces would be built in the middle of the woods! If the building had chimneys made of straw and plaster like the ones in Jamestown, then there could be fires—forest fires!

Nat was terrified. Had the London Company thought of this possibility? His fears of fire returned. He went weak thinking about the fire in London.

The only person Nat had ever been able to talk to about the loss of his family was Vicar Hunt. He had understood and had tried to make Nat realize that he was bigger than anything that could ever happen to him, but that it took strength of character to overcome sorrow, hardship and disappointment. Nat recalled that Master Hunt had said: "Son, you must work hard. You must strive to become a better boy, physically and spiritually. Disappointment and sorrow can build you, if you will only let them."

But Nat found it difficult, especially now that he didn't have the minister's guidance.

His imagination went wild.

The foreigners, the glassmakers, would be trapped if a fire started in the forest. They might even be burned to death! John had said the glass house had to be in the forest because the furnaces would use so much wood. Why couldn't it be built in a clearing away from the forest and the wood hauled to the house? If Vicar Hunt were alive, he might persuade the council not to build the glass house in the woods. How Nat wished he were old enough to be a member of the council!

These Germans and Poles who had come over to Virginia were sincere in their purpose. They were not like the neer-do-well venturers. They wanted to build a glass house and to make glass—something that could grow and grow and could be permanent. Maybe glass making, the first skilled industry in America, would make Jamestown famous!

Captain Smith's words rang in his ears. "What we need is quality—men who have trades. Not quantity—men who are only seeking adventure! We can't feed them, and it means more of us will die!" Jamestown was desperate for men who were willing to work and build a permanent settlement.

As Nat looked out the open door, he saw dozens of poorly built cabins with triangle-like roofs. They had been constructed hastily of green wood and already they were sagging. Now that the wood had dried out, the situation was even more serious. There were big cracks that let in the cold air. They were nothing like the solid stone buildings in England. Westminister Abbey and the Tower of London would last for centuries, maybe forever.

Nat had never thought about this before in relation to Jamestown. The houses could fall down or burn any moment. And there was so much talk of gold buzzing through men's minds that little had been done about clearing the ground for gardens and fields. But he mustn't think any more about those things. There was work in the kitchen waiting for him.

A few mornings later Nat got up at dawn as usual to feed Mattie. He had looked for Tomo, but did not see him. Nat knew, however, he would appear later. He smiled as he thought about the Indian boy. Tomo was independent and knew far better than anyone else at

Jamestown how to take care of himself. At least Nat didn't have to worry about him.

While the raccoon greedily ate her fish, having first dipped it in the hollow log Tomo had made for her, Nat sat inside the pen studying the clay model. He sighed heavily. The clay as he had molded it didn't resemble Mattie in any way. In fact, it didn't look like any animal he had ever seen.

Suddenly he was aware of someone standing over him. A man had come upon him so quietly that Nat hadn't heard him.

The man smiled, *"Guten tag,"* he said kindly. Then slowly, in labored English, he asked, "What are you making?" He pointed to the clay model Nat held firmly in his right hand.

"A raccoon," Nat answered. "Mattie is my pet."

The man looked at Mattie and laughed. He seemed fascinated by her and Nat recalled how pleased Tomo had been with Mattie the first time he had seen her.

"Funny! I have never seen animal like it." He laughed again. It was contagious and Nat laughed with him.

The man squatted beside Nat and looked at the clay model. "You make?" he asked.

Nat nodded.

"Of animal."

Nat nodded again.

"It is hard. You are good."

"No, I'm not," Nat answered quickly.

"You try very hard."

This man seemed to understand. Nat wanted to know more about him. "I'm Nat Pecock," he said. "What is your name? Aren't you a glassmaker?"

The man nodded. "Felix Stanislaw. I help you, if you like," he said modestly.

Nat held out his crude attempt. Felix took it and began pressing the clay firmly but carefully. How swiftly he worked! With each motion, the clay looked more like the raccoon. Felix shaped a pointed nose and then tiny ears.

"Why, that's Mattie!" Nat said enthusiastically.

"You had started right," Felix smiled. "Would you like to work in the glass house?" he asked abruptly.

"Why do you ask me?" Nat was puzzled.

"You have art," the man nodded. "You love beauty."

Nat smiled.

Felix continued. "We need men to work with beauty."

"But Governor Smith says I must work in the kitchen," he said aloud.

Felix ignored Nat's remark. "I teach you. You do well. You could be my apprentice. You are young. Maybe you have a future as glassblower."

"I don't want to work all my life in the kitchen," Nat said rebelliously. "But Captain Smith says I must. I don't know how I could make him change his mind."

"You have good friends?" Felix asked.

"John Laydon is my good friend, but he isn't on the council."

"A way will come if you want it badly enough," Felix said, and started to leave. "But you must work. *Auf Wiederschen.*"

That was the way Vicar Hunt had talked to him! "I must prove to Captain Smith how very much I want to work in the glass house," Nat said, looking hopefully toward the settlement.

8

At Work in the Woods

NAT KNEW Captain Newport was faced with many problems. When the council announced that the glass house would be located about a mile from the fort, the real trouble started. The Poles and Germans were afraid of the Indians and a sudden attack.

"Thousands of Indians live close to Jamestown," the colonists had warned them, in a deliberate attempt to scare them. "We never know when they'll surprise the settlement, set fire to the fort and scalp us!"

The glassmakers had never even seen an Indian until they arrived in Virginia. Fear ran among them.

That very afternoon Nat took Tomo to the cabin where Felix Stanislaw and the glassblowers were staying, hoping that if they knew one good Indian, they might be less afraid.

"Hello," Nat said when the Pole came to the door. "I brought my best friend, Tomocomo, here to meet you and the other men."

Felix shook hands with the willowy Indian boy and smiled. Then he beckoned to the other seven Poles and Germans who also shook hands with Tomo. They greeted him with *"Guten Tag."*

Tomo said, "Good day."

Because they didn't understand the same language, it made it almost impossible for the men and the Indian boy to talk.

Later, as they walked away, Tomo said, "They are good. I like their faces."

"Felix said they liked you," Nat said.

"I hope so," Tomo smiled.

Word had just come from Werowocomoco that Chief Powhatan liked Thomas Savage and that the English boy was learning the Indian customs and language.

Nat turned to Tomo. "Do you want to go back to your village?" he asked.

Tomo shook his head.

"Why not?" Nat asked.

"I have you. We have Matoaka," he said. "I am learning white man's language to help my people. We want to be friends."

The glassmakers did not want to live near the glass house, but the older settlers had more influence. So the decision was made that lodgings would be built for the Germans and Poles at Glass House Point.

"It will be better for you," one colonist tried to assure the men. "You'll only be a mile from the fort."

Nat guessed that the Englishmen didn't want the Poles and Germans living inside the fort with them. This worried him. He liked the glassmakers. Maybe when the Germans and Poles knew more English and could talk more easily with them, the settlers would feel differently. He hoped so very much.

Because of Felix, Nat now had a real interest. He was experimenting with clay. There was something wonderful about a piece of clay. When it was dug out of the ground, it seemed like any other kind of earth. But after Nat had cupped it in his hands and it became pliable, he loved to form it into a ball. All the time he kneaded it, pounding out the air, he wondered what form it would eventually take.

Nat admired Felix's deft touch. Felix encouraged him so he knew he was doing good work. Felix made a wooden board for him and demonstrated the way to add bits of clay to the original piece for ears and feet. He even loaned Nat some of his priceless tools that he had brought over with him. After many long hours, Nat was finally satisfied with his raccoon model, and so was his teacher.

"I can hardly wait until you fire it," Nat said. "After it is baked in the kiln, it will be firm."

"Just as soon as the big oven is finished, I'll do it," Felix answered.

When they started to build the glass house, the venturers objected to the steady work and long hours. Nat was sorry that the example set by the industrious Germans and Poles didn't carry over to the others. Instead, it produced more friction than ever.

A half-dozen men were assigned to dig the well. The clay they dug out of the hole was hauled to the glass house where it would be used for the furnaces. The hole for the well was dug a foot or two below the normal ground water level. Then a large wooden barrel, nearly four feet tall and made with oak staves held together with iron hoops, was set in the bottom of the hole.

Nat noticed that the heaviest work was unloading the boulders from the two-ton barge tied to the cypress trees along the bank of the river. They would use these stones for the furnaces. Some of the men had taken the barge up the James to get the "great cobble stones," as Captain Newport had described them in his report to the London Company more than a year before. The boulders were in the outcroppings at the falls.

Since Nat had never had the chance to go on any of these expeditions, he was interested in the limestone boulders. Some were small, rounded ones only about five or six inches across. Others were large, irregular ones as much as two feet long.

Nat wondered why they had gone so far from the fort to get them. He had seen identical boulders on the bars and beaches of the river where they had been washed down by flood waters.

When he asked Captain Newport about this, the captain answered, "There's a great supply near the falls. Since we could float the barge so close to the shore line, it saved the men's time and energy."

The glassmakers knew the kind of building they needed. John Laydon helped construct it.

"The glass house will be about thirty-seven by fifty feet," John told Nat. "It will be a simple framework of logs, resting on timber supports. We're using lumber from trees that are curved to make the A frames. Right now we're waiting for the men to make more tree nails. Those wooden pegs of dry compressed timber will swell in the holes when moistened. It should be a sturdy building."

Nat was impressed that John knew so much about construction.

Nowadays he hurried through his work in the kitchen as quickly as possible so he could go out to the glass house.

"You can run faster than a deer when you want to," Tomo said to him one morning. "And walk as slow as a turtle when you don't want to."

"That's right," Nat laughed. "See you later. I'm going to fly like a bird right now, a mile a minute."

Nat tried his best to interest Tomo in what the men were doing. But Tomo was indifferent.

Nat had noticed a change in Tomo ever since he and Felix had become good friends, especially now that Felix was teaching him so much about modeling. Nat decided that Tomo wanted to be free to roam in the woods whenever he felt like it. In many ways Tomo was like a wild animal. However, Nat had to admit that the Indian boy had more patience than he had when making a bow and arrow, but he became restless when Nat urged him to try to make something from clay.

"Work too slow. Too much like squaw work," Tomo said emphatically.

Now Nat could laugh about squaw work. It didn't bother him as it had at first.

Nat's duties were still in the kitchen and nothing had been said yet about his working in the glass house. But somehow he felt his chance would come. He still knew he would have to convince Captain Newport and Governor Smith but he had not yet figured out a plan.

Nat tried not to become too impatient and discouraged. If he worked hard at the job which had been assigned to him, then at least the two leaders could not find fault with him.

One afternoon when Nat was watching the men work and really envying them, John Laydon walked over to him.

"Well, Nat," he said, pointing to the building, "we're about ready to cover the two sides facing the river. We've already mixed the straw and mud, so now we can dab it on. The men have almost finished placing the rods or wattle on the roof. That will support the thatch. The next step is to put the reeds which we've gathered from the swamp on the roof. They've been tied with vines and are stacked up over there." He nodded toward them. "We want a strong house because there has to be protection from the cold winds and rains that sweep down from the river."

"Are you building chimneys in the glass house?" Nat asked. He still couldn't get the awful fear of fire out of his mind.

John shook his head. "No. But there are openings in the roof to let smoke and heat escape."

"But . . ." Nat started to reason with John, then decided that it would be useless. John was following the plans that had been decided by the London Company in faraway England. This meant that there would be an even greater danger of fire!

The one advantage was that if only the two sides that faced the James were enclosed, the men would not be trapped in case of fire with only one exit to the building. That was the way his family had perished.

When the large shed was completed, the well dug, and

the boulders for the furnaces were piled near the glass house, Captain Newport seemed less tense.

"The London Company demands so much," Nat heard him tell Governor Smith.

"Much too much," Governor Smith answered. "When you sail back to England, I'm sending a letter to them. It will be a strong protest. This ship with the second supply did not have adequate provisions in the hold. Our men are not farmers. We haven't raised enough this past summer to keep us in food for the winter. We should be making arrangements with the Indians to barter for corn."

"You must leave soon to invite Powhatan here to be crowned," Captain Newport said. "He will be so honored by that and the gifts that he'll generously give us all the maize the colony will need for a long time."

Governor Smith shook his head, pulling on his red beard. "I don't agree with you."

"You never agree with me!" Captain Newport shrugged his shoulders and walked rapidly away.

Nat wondered which captain was right. Nat had been through that starving period with Captain Smith when so many had died. The ones who had lived still considered it a miracle that they had been spared. He never wanted that terrible experience again. Another time they might be forced to abandon the colony. Then his hope for a permanent place in America would be gone, maybe forever.

But Nat realized that his only chance to do the kind of work he really wanted to do rested with the glass house. So in a way he was as eager as Captain Newport was for the Germans and Poles to make their first glass samples.

Felix explained to Nat that the stone walls of the working furnace, the main oven, had to be thick to save heat. The arched dome over the melting chamber had to be built as low as possible to bring the flames down close to the tops of the melting pots.

"What are melting pots?" Nat asked.

Felix laughed. "That's right, you don't know much about glassmaking, but I hope you will soon." He thought for a moment. "When you boil venison over the fire, you need a pot to put the meat and water in. Well, when we make glass we have to have large vessels to hold the mixture of sand, soda and lime. We call them melting pots. They can hold from sixty-five to one hundred and forty-five pounds of melted glass. But these pots have to go far inside the oven, not on top of the furnace."

"What shape are they?" Nat asked. He really was interested.

"Round like a half-moon," Felix answered. "The melting pots sit on *sieges* or seats inside the furnace. These supports are about one foot above the floor of the chamber where the fire is burning."

"How do you get to these melting pots?" Nat asked. He was suddenly full of questions.

"There will be a large opening at the back of the furnace," Felix explained. "Normally the opening is kept blocked up with clay, but when a pot goes to pieces in the furnace, which often happens, we dig out the temporary filling and replace the pot without having to cut down the heat in the furnace." He paused. "Replacing broken pots is one of the most troublesome problems of glassmaking, and I guess it always will be." Felix sighed, then went on. "We brought over a few pots along with our tools, so that we could get started as soon as the furnaces are finished. I hope that the sand and clay here in Virginia are better than what we've been using in Europe. If that is the case, we may be able to make finer glass articles and stronger clay pots than the Italians."

"I can hardly wait to watch you make glass," Nat said.

"I'm expecting you to be my apprentice any day now."

Nat shook his head. "That may not be possible. I can't figure out how to convince the two captains."

"You will," Felix nodded.

At least Nat had several friends who believed in him.

"The working holes in the furnace," Felix continued, "will not only mean we can get to the hot glass easily, but we can reheat the glass as it is being worked."

"This all sounds so hard," Nat wrinkled his forehead.

"Wait until I can show you," Felix smiled, "and I will as soon as the furnaces are ready."

9

Nat Appeals to the Governor

IN THE EARLY HOURS after the sun rose, Nat watched the men line up like soldiers and march out of the fort. Some headed for the forest to chop down trees for clapboards and to build the glass house. Others toiled in the tar pits.

The men chafed under the strict orders given by both Captain Newport and Governor Smith. They wanted to choose their work. Nat didn't feel quite so resentful now about his own chores because the whole settlement was under this iron hand.

About the only time Captain Newport and Governor Smith seemed to agree was when the men were working hard.

"At this rate," Nat heard Captain Newport tell the governor, "there will be paying goods to load on the ship when I return to England in December."

"The London Company may be satisfied with what we're doing," the governor answered, "but this isn't helping us get our own food supplies. We have a long winter ahead of us."

One day when the boys were feeding Mattie, Nat mentioned to Tomo that there was hardly any corn left in the storehouse. "Maybe that's why Governor Smith is so cross," he said. "He wants to send men out on trading expeditions to barter for maize with your people, but the captain insists that making glass and building up the piles of clapboard are more important."

"If my people didn't have maize, they would starve," Tomo said. "White people need maize, too."

"There are too many mouths to feed," Nat said. "The governor worries about this, I know. If there isn't enough food, some of us will die," he added soberly.

"People should not have to be hungry," Tomo said slowly. "Maize grows in many places."

Nat hadn't expected Tomo to be so concerned about this problem in Jamestown. They were both quiet as they watched Mattie eat. Later they walked through the forest back to the fort without saying a word.

Nat knew he had to ask Governor Smith for the chance to work in the glass house, but he dreaded it. When he talked to John Laydon, his friend felt he should ask the governor, but added, "I'm not the one to intercede for you. I'm not on the council."

"If good Master Hunt were only here!" Nat sighed.

"We all miss him," John said kindly. "His faith in life kept us all going. It was his devoted example that prevented quarrels and dissensions on board ship. If it hadn't been for him the project of establishing a colony in this new country would have been abandoned before we even landed."

"I guess I'll have to convince Governor Smith myself," Nat said slowly.

"It's your only chance, Nat," John agreed.

As Nat walked across the square, he made a face at the cabin where so much of the time he felt like a prisoner chained to routine kitchen chores. He had delayed long enough. He would ask Governor Smith before the day was over.

That evening, after his chores were finished, Nat knocked on the door of the governor's cabin. Through the open window he saw him working on a large piece of parchment. Nat guessed it was the map of Virginia that he had drawn himself.

"Come in," Governor Smith called out.

Nat walked in and stood in front of the table. The governor did not look up. He was measuring something on the parchment.

"Governor Smith." Nat's voice trembled.

"Yes." Governor Smith raised his hand.

"You need men to work in the glass house?" Then he hesitated. "I–I'd like to have you consider me. I want to learn how to make glass."

"You have a good job," Governor Smith said. "You're better off where you are."

"There's no future in the kitchen," Nat persisted. "There could be a real job for me at the glass house. I am a good worker."

"The men who make bottles, windowpanes and other glass articles are trained," Governor Smith said. "They are craftsmen. You haven't had that training. You know how to manage the kitchen. In fact, you're about the only one who can. We have to eat. We need you where you are."

Nat realized that the governor was trying to pay him a compliment, but it made him no happier about his kitchen work. He opened his mouth to tell him that Felix Stanislaw wanted him to be his apprentice, but the governor went on talking.

He looked sternly at Nat. "Have you forgotten so soon His Majestie's Council for Virginia?" he asked. " 'The way to prosper and achieve good success is to make yourselves all of one mind for the good of your country and your own.' "

That settled it. Governor Smith intended to keep him in the kitchen.

"Good night, Nathaniel," the governor said as he picked up his quill.

"Good evening, Governor Smith," the disappointed boy said politely.

Nat opened the door slowly and went out into the dark night. He was more discouraged than he had ever been. His feet dragged as he walked past the other buildings. He couldn't go back to his own cabin and face the men. He wanted to see Mattie.

As he approached the entrance to the south gate, a guard called out: "Who goes there?"

"Nat Pecock, sir," the boy answered.

"No one is to leave the settlement after dark," said the guard.

"But it's important. I want to see Mattie," Nat pleaded. "She needs her supper."

"Who's Mattie?" the guard asked as he adjusted the musket from the left shoulder to his right.

"My pet raccoon."

"No, you can't go," the guard said. "We have strict orders from the president of the council. I repeat, no one can leave the fort after dark."

Nat knew he couldn't disobey the order.

His feet dragged more than ever as he turned toward the cabin. He hadn't got anywhere with Governor Smith. Now, because of this new rule, he couldn't even tell Mattie about his disappointment. Just having her snuggle up to him would have reassured him that at least the raccoon still loved him. Nat suddenly felt lonely. He had no idea where Tomo was, but even he wouldn't understand how he felt.

Nat consoled himself with the thought that he'd get up before dawn and go out to Mattie's pen.

As he approached the Forrest cabin, the candlelight inside seemed to be glowing brighter than he had ever noticed before. He paused in front of the house, wanting to enter.

While he stood there, Ann Burras and John Laydon returned from a short walk. Every time Nat saw Ann he liked her better. She had such a pleasant manner. He had seen John and Ann walking together rather often of late. He hoped this meant that John was seriously interested in her. John was a fine man and he worked hard as a carpenter.

"Hello, Nat," Ann Burras greeted him. "Where are you going?"

"Back to my cabin," Nat answered, hanging his head.

"Wouldn't you like to come in and visit with us for a while?" she asked in a friendly tone. "We might have some tea and cake."

"Thank you." Nat looked up. "I'd like to very much." The three went into the house together.

The Forrests greeted Nat, Mistress Forrest offering him a stool to sit on. How pleasant it was to be with these nice people. Nat was aware of homey touches Mistress Forrest and Ann had brought to the room that made it more comfortable. What a contrast to the bare cabin where he slept.

Over the stone fireplace pans glistened. Nat never took the extra time to shine the kettles after he had washed them. He felt guilty when he saw how attractive bright pans were.

Nat decided that he would not tell John now about his disappointment. He'd tell him another time.

"Felix Stanislaw has promised to make windowpanes for me," Mistress Forrest said cheerily, "just as soon as he can."

"And I'll make pretty curtains for you," Ann offered.

Nat listened to the women's musical voices. He was fascinated by the rustle of their full skirts. Mistress Forrest was gracious, but Ann was especially lovely.

He looked over at John who seemed content and relaxed. Nat noticed how often he smiled at Ann.

As Nat drank the tea and ate the delicious cake, he thought of his own family. His mother had liked to cook and she used to make cake that melted in his mouth. There was one cup in their home that was decorated with roses that his mother had called, "Nat's big cup." The tea tasted so good in that special cup. Nat sighed. If only he could have a home again!

Suddenly he thought of Mattie. Had something happened to her? Surely everything was all right. It had been up to now.

"I must leave," Nat said suddenly. "It's getting late and I have to get up before dawn." He stood up, looking at his friends. "Thank you for asking me to your home."

"Please come often," Mistress Forrest said as she opened the door.

He would have gone immediately from the cottage to

check on his raccoon if he could have slipped past the guard, but that was impossible. He couldn't understand why he was so concerned about Mattie. If Tomo would only sleep in the same cabin with him, instead of on a bed of evergreens in the forest, he could share his anxiety with him.

10

The Governor Relents

NAT WOKE UP several times in the night. His dreams were disturbed and frightening. He relived the scene with the governor when he refused to let him work in the glass house. After one dream where Mattie had been caught by a fox, it was impossible for him to go back to sleep. When dawn finally came, Nat was waiting impatiently at the south entrance of the fort for the guard to unlock the gate. He had to see Mattie and be sure that she was all right.

He had never run so fast before down the forest trails. His voice echoed through the woods, "Mattie! Mattie!"

But no raccoon squealed her happy greeting when he arrived at the pen. He searched behind the big oak, where Mattie sometimes hid when she played hide and seek with the two boys. He looked up in her favorite tree and even in the water trough, the hollow log Tomo had made for her. But Mattie was not in her pen.

Finally Nat found a small opening in the wooden fence. She must have squeezed through the hole. But why had she run away?

He hurried to the bank of the river, hoping she was there catching fish for her breakfast. He ran a mile or so up and down the bank, farther than Mattie had ever gone. Then he raced back to the pen, hoping desperately that she had come back. But Mattie wasn't there.

Before he left, he placed a stone against the door to keep it ajar. If Mattie returned, at least she wouldn't have any trouble getting back into her pen. He put fresh water in the hollow log and even pulled up some roots, the kind the raccoon especially liked. Since he couldn't find her collar, he decided that it must still be around her neck.

After searching again in the forest and calling "Mattie" until his voice was hoarse, he reluctantly turned back toward the fort. He had his regular chores that he didn't dare neglect. The men had to have breakfast before they started their long day of hard work.

By this time Nat was also worried about Tomo. Where was the Indian boy? He had never been gone so long before.

During the day, whenever he had any free time, Nat hurried to the forest and called Mattie and Tomo. The only sounds were the echoes, "Eee" and "Ooo," that came back faintly. Why was it suddenly so still, and why weren't there more small animals about? Perhaps they were hiding or sleeping.

He needed Tomo now more than ever. Surely he would know where to look for the raccoon, especially if she were hiding somewhere in the woods. Nat was certain no one had stolen her. But it disturbed him that Mattie had wanted to run away.

When Nat talked to John about his two losses, his friend tried to reassure him. "Mattie will come back, and so will Tomo."

Nat wasn't at all certain. Mattie had once lived in the forest. Maybe she was lonely for other raccoons. Perhaps he should try to catch another and raise two pets.

But the puzzle about Tomo's disappearance remained. The Indian boy liked living at the settlement. They were friends and Nat felt that Tomo would have told him if he intended to return to his own village. Why did he leave?

Nat's unhappiness filled him with fear. The bad dream about the raccoon still troubled him.

As he walked slowly back to the fort for the last time that afternoon, one of the guards said, "Governor Smith has been looking for you. Go at once to his cabin." It was a command.

"Why does he want to see me?" Nat asked.

"I don't know," the guard answered gruffly. "Those are his orders."

Nat didn't hurry. One of the settlers stopped him. "Did you find the Indian boy?" he asked.

Nat shook his head. So word had already spread that Tomo had gone away.

"You won't," the man said. "I knew that Indian wouldn't stay with us long. He's gone back to his village. Indians are all the same. They're cunning and treacherous. All this time he's been spying on us."

"Tomo is my best friend," Nat said loyally. "He isn't a spy."

"Oh no?" the man scoffed. "We can expect an Indian attack any day now."

How suspicious people were! Nat was certain Tomo would not spy on the white settlers at Jamestown or harm them in any way. But other people didn't think that. They didn't know Tomo.

As Nat entered the cabin he could see the governor was angry. "Nathaniel Pecock, I've been waiting for you," he snapped.

"I'm sorry I couldn't get here before," Nat said respectfully. He couldn't tell Captain Smith about his troubles.

Nat glanced at the table where the governor sat. There was his clay raccoon! Nat had thought it was with his few personal belongings in the cabin, along with the *Book of Common Prayer*. What was it doing here?

The governor picked up the little clay animal. "I understand you made this." His voice was still sharp.

"Yes," Nat nodded. "But Felix Stanislaw helped me. I never could have made the clay look like the raccoon without him."

"Captain Newport and Master Stanislaw came to see me this morning," Governor Smith said, as he pulled on his beard. He had placed the model back on the table. "Master Stanislaw needs an apprentice. He has asked me if I will permit you to be his, to learn the art of glassmaking."

Nat couldn't believe his ears! At last he was to have his chance!

Before he could answer, the governor spoke again. "It's

a long training period, Nathaniel." He paused. "Are you sure you want to be a glassblower? The glass house is a new venture. It may not succeed. But the only way it will is to have good workmen. There are so few among the colonists who are interested in this industry. You're young. You should learn a trade."

Why had Governor Smith changed his mind about him so quickly? Nat watched him examine the clay raccoon. He turned it at various angles, apparently greatly interested.

"You seem to have special talent, my boy. That counts for a great deal."

Nat still couldn't believe this was happening to him. He had waited so long.

"However," the governor continued, "it's impossible to let you work full time at the glass house. There are duties in the kitchen that are just as important. But we'll try you out for about five hours a day with Felix Stanislaw. That means you will still have your chores, but not quite so many. You can start with Master Stanislaw as his apprentice tomorrow morning. Good night." And a nod of the governor's head dismissed Nat.

"Thank you, Governor Smith," Nat said gratefully. Once outside, he ran to tell John.

11

Apprentice at Last

THE RUMOR THAT Captain Newport would set out soon with an expedition to search for gold and the Lost Colony on Roanoke Island, as well as to look for a way to the western sea, spread rapidly through the settlement. If the captain had intended to keep it a secret until he was ready to pick the men, his plans hadn't worked out. The venturers were impatient to leave. They shouted loud approval when they learned that at least one hundred would go on the expedition.

Again Nat felt disappointed. He wanted to go with them on this searching party even more than he wanted to be an apprentice. But it was too late now. He was committed as an apprentice to Felix.

"The governor had to get some workers to replace the men at the glass house," Nat complained to John. "That's why I got this chance, not because he thinks I have any special talent."

"Don't jump to conclusions so fast," John said calmly. "Be grateful that you will be working and learning a valuable skill."

"But now I'll never get to look for gold," Nat said bitterly.

"A young man has to decide sometime what road he wants to follow," John said. "Do you want to follow the uncertain path of gold that will probably lead to nowhere, or do you want to follow the one that will give you a trade in a business that is new in this country and has a real future?"

Nat nodded a bit uncertainly. His friend knew better than he what he really wanted.

Nat realized why these venturers were excited. They had waited a long time and far from patiently for the order. Captain Newport intended to find the valuable ore if any existed in Virginia. A hundred men could do a lot of digging around the countryside. The London Company wanted gold and this seemed the easiest way to get it. If this expedition were successful, then Jamestown would be a money-making colony.

It was no secret to the colonists that Governor Smith disapproved of this expedition. He considered Captain Newport's demand for one hundred men a foolish waste. Also, it would leave scarcely enough settlers to guard the fort and to work on the products that would sell for good prices in England. But Captain Newport ranked above

Governor Smith, so he was forced to go along with his superior's plans.

That first day as he entered the glass house, Nat felt strange. He hadn't been inside the building since it was finished, but John had kept him informed of the progress.

Smoke from the furnaces filled the big room. Nat blinked as his eyes began to smart. The gray haze partially blinded him and he couldn't see the glassblower.

"Felix," he called.

"Hello, Nat," the glassblower answered cheerfully as he came over to greet him. "Not crying, are you?" he chuckled.

"I can't see." Nat's eyes watered and tears rolled down his cheeks. He wiped his eyes. "I have good news. Governor Smith says I can be your apprentice and I'm to start work right now!"

"That's fine," Felix smiled. "I need you. Captain Newport intends to take some of my best men for his gold expedition. But first you'll have to learn about the furnaces and the names of the tools we use."

Nat saw four oblong masses of rocks. Those were the furnaces. He also noticed tubs of water, piles of sand and a wooden box of oyster shells, as well as another box filled with lime. He looked more closely at the main furnace, but he couldn't find a chimney. When Nat asked Felix why, he said: "There can't be a chimney in the furnace. It is important, as I explained to you once before, that the flames and combustion gasses be drawn around and over the melting pots which are inside." He pointed to some openings in the furnace. "Those working holes serve as the main draft flues."

Felix showed him one in the crown of the largest furnace. "That hole is made large enough so that we can replace the broken pots. This is also where we reheat the glass as we work on it. When one of the pots for melting the glass goes to pieces in the furnace, we take the temporary filling out of the large opening in the back of the furnace." Felix pointed to that section. To Nat it looked the same as the other part of the furnace, except that the stones seemed loose.

"Then we put the pot in," Felix went on. "This way we can replace it without having to cut down the heat of the furnace too much. One of these days you'll learn how to replace the pots."

Since there were four furnaces in the room, Nat assumed that they were all used for the same purpose. But he found out that such was not the case.

"In this small furnace or kiln," Felix explained, "we fire the new melting pots. They have a short life, so this furnace will be used a great deal to make more of the melting pots to hold the glass." Felix showed Nat where there was just enough room at the back of the kiln for a platform to hold one pot. It was also used to preheat pots before putting them in the working furnace.

They walked over a little farther on so that Nat could see another furnace. A man who had been mixing sand, lime and potash together, was now ready to place the dry materials on the floor of the furnace. "We'll heat this just enough to produce a partial fusion without actually melting the glass," Felix explained. "This is the fritting furnace."

It was a new word for Nat, so he listened carefully to everything the glassblower said.

"Later we'll shovel or rake the glassy substance or hot frit, for that's what it's called, out of the opening near the back of the furnace onto the platform."

They walked over to the wooden boxes. Nat recognized the sand that men had brought from the nearby river bank. Some of the lime had come from oyster shells. Nat had seen the settlers collect these shells and use them to make mortar and plaster after they had been pounded fine. The ship also had brought a supply of lime. "It was ground up, though, before we shipped the lime," Felix said.

"Now that the furnaces are going, we have plenty of ashes," Felix went on. "It's good the glass house is in the forest, because the furnaces really burn the wood." He took Nat over to one side of the glass house where there were pans of water. "We make the potash which we need for glass by putting ashes into these pans of water and allowing the water to evaporate. This leaves a crude product. But until we are making glass on a bigger scale, this is satisfactory for *waldglas.*"

"What's that?" Nat asked.

"I forgot," Felix laughed. "In German we call it *waldglas,* but in English it's common green glass. The first glass we made turned out fair. But as we experiment with this native sand, we soon will be able to produce a better glass."

There was so much to learn! Nat wondered whether he could ever master the art of glassmaking.

Nat heard Felix say, "Then of course we also use old glass or *cullet.*" He had never thought of that. "We break so much glass in the process of making it. So gradually we are accumulating more cullet."

Felix looked at Nat. "The founder, the man who handles our fritting furnace, will soon be pulled off his job to go on the gold expedition. I'll be handling the *calcar,* or fritting furnace, for a while, and I want you to learn that part of glassmaking." He paused. "Is that all right with you?"

"Of course." Nat nodded. It was a wonderful feeling to be considered, instead of being ordered.

"Then we might as well get started," the glassblower said.

Nat and Felix mixed sand, which Nat shoveled from the sandbox. They added lime, potash and soda. All this was shoveled onto the ledge at the back of the *calcar*. As the heat rose, Felix, now working as the founder in charge of the fritting furnace, stirred the mixture and worked it over with a long-handled rake.

Nat admired the way Felix handled the tool, and he noted how particular he was about mixing the materials.

"Your motions are so even," Nat said. The glassblower looked up and smiled. Nat thought that Felix had a faraway look, as though he were thinking of something that had happened in the past.

"I had a good teacher when I was an apprentice," he smiled. "I hope I'll be able to do as well with you as the master did for me." He paused. "The master loved making beautiful things and he inspired me to strive for perfection and graceful lines." He turned abruptly. "It's time for you to rake," he said and handed Nat the tool.

Nat stirred the mixture and worked it over as he had seen Felix do, aware he was being watched.

A minute later Felix picked up the long-handled hoe and started pulling the stuff out of the furnace and onto the stone platform. He worked fast, not saying a word. When he finished, Felix wiped his forehead with the back of his hand.

"That is the art," he said. "At the right moment you must know when the frit must come out. It cannot get too hot. It had reached the proper stage and I was so busy I couldn't take time to explain to you what I was doing."

"I tried to watch everything you did," Nat said.

"You look as if you have good eyes," Felix smiled. "I hoped you watched carefully, because as soon as possible I want you to be in charge of this furnace."

What a contrast to his kitchen chores! Did Felix mean he would promote him as fast as he mastered each phase of glassmaking?

"Now we'll let this semifused mixture cool," Felix said, pointing down to the grayish stuff. "Later we'll break it up and store it away."

Nat followed the glassblower to the entrance of the factory. The sunlight cut sharply through the smoke. As they leaned against the building, Nat took deep breaths of fresh air.

"While the explorers are away," Felix said, "we will be shorthanded. I'm worried because Captain Newport wants a goodly supply of glass articles to ship back." He shook his head. "But he's not consistent. He wants us to make glass, but he plans to take some of our best men."

Nat nodded.

"There's only one bright spot," Felix went on, "and that is that the Germans and Poles who go on that expedition will probably be forced to learn English. I haven't been of much help. Even though I know more than most of them do, I'd rather talk to the men in my own tongue." He laughed. "I've talked more English today than ever before. Now that you are working with me, I hope you'll help me learn."

"You speak it well," Nat said. "I'd like to learn German," he hinted.

"If we all knew Indian, English and German we might get along better here in Virginia," Felix said thoughtfully. "Since we are to be shorthanded, why don't you persuade Tomo to work with you in the glass house?"

Nat would have welcomed the chance to ask Tomo but he didn't know where the Indian boy was. This was the second day he and Mattie had been away.

"Tomo's not here right now," Nat said, "but I'll ask him as soon as I can."

While Felix had explained the art of glassmaking to him, Nat for the first time in the last few days had forgotten about his two losses. Now he remembered them. Once again he was miserable.

"I like that boy," Felix said, "and he's loyal to you."

Nat sighed silently. At least Felix had not heard the rumor that Tomo was a spy who had deserted the white people to return to his Indian village!

"Tomo is bright, and he's thoughtful," Nat said. "He loves the raccoon as much as I do."

"Those are good qualities in any boy," Felix nodded.

How glad he was to hear Felix talk like this. Felix liked Tomo. That was important.

When they stopped at noon to eat their lunch of bread and meat, Nat decided to ask Felix about some problems that troubled him. When he told him about Tomo's disappearance, Felix thought a moment and then said: "He may have gone back to his village for a visit, but I think he'll return." He scratched his blond beard. "Something may be troubling him," he said thoughtfully.

"Tomo doesn't talk much, but I never thought he had any problems."

"We all worry, but some of us keep our worries to ourselves," Felix said. "Maybe Tomo is troubled about something that has happened here in Jamestown."

Nat hadn't thought of that. "Then you don't think he ran away and won't come back?" Nat asked. He needed reassurance on this point.

"No. There must be a good reason why Tomo left

without telling you. But I think he'll be back in a few days. If he is the loyal friend you say he is, and I think so, he will come back when he has solved the problem." Felix looked out toward the dense forest. "Who knows? Maybe he is hunting for Mattie?"

"I hope he finds her." Nat said.

Vicar Hunt would have given him just the same kind of sympathetic explanation that Felix had, Nat thought. John Laydon had also assured him that Tomo and Mattie would come back. If these men thought so, there was still hope.

12

The Wanderers Return

As NAT APPROACHED the south entrance of the palisaded fort that evening at sundown, he was surprised to see some of the English settlers who had been living upriver near the falls. Several had already crowded through the gate, holding their bundles tightly.

Nat hurried. "What's happened?" he asked as he reached the gate. One of the men who was sitting on his pack, his shoulders drooping, turned to Nat. He looked exhausted and his face was drawn and tired looking.

"The Indians have forced most of us to leave our village at Nansemond and the falls," he answered, shaking his head. "We've never been so frightened. We grabbed what few belongings we have and hurried to the fort as soon as we could. Here at least the cannons will protect us. But the boy, Samuel Collier, is still at the falls."

Nat realized the colonists lived in constant fear of the Indians. He recalled the first Indian attack shortly after they had arrived in May, 1607. One boy had been killed and seventeen men injured. That first year the Indians had often lain in wait, hiding in the long grasses outside the palisades, to shoot an arrow into an unwary white man. But recently there had been no trouble.

This was alarming news. Did it mean the Indians were warning them of future trouble? As Nat listened to the settlers, he wondered whether there might be an attack.

The fact that Tomo still had not returned troubled him again.

"That Indian boy you've been friendly with is a spy," the guard said to Nat as he shouldered his musket. "Now we're sure of it. He's not only learned our language but he's spotted the weaknesses of our fort."

What could Nat say? He decided it was useless to argue with the guard. He wouldn't be able to convince the man that his friend was not a spy. At least Felix and John didn't think Tomo was a bad Indian, and their opinions meant much to Nat.

By this time most of the colonists had assembled in the clearing inside the fort. Nat stood close to John and Ann. Captain Newport turned to Governor Smith. "You must leave immediately for Werowocomoco and invite Chief Powhatan to Jamestown to be crowned and to receive his presents. He will be so honored that he will not allow any of his warriors to attack us."

Captain Newport gave this order with confidence. At least Nat didn't think from the tone of his voice that he was as worried about an Indian attack as were the frightened settlers.

Captain Newport turned to the assembled men and two women. "This means we will delay the expedition until after the coronation."

The men nodded and talked among themselves. Nat was surprised that the adventurers accepted the decision. For once they seemed to understand that there was a greater need elsewhere.

"I'll start at dawn tomorrow," Governor Smith said. "Four men will go with me. We'll travel by land north to the Pamunkey River and then continue by canoe to Chief Powhatan's village."

The following morning Nat was at the glass house early, mixing sand, potash, soda and lime. He was about ready to put it in the fritting furnace when he felt a tap on his shoulder. He turned around quickly. There was Tomo holding Mattie. Beside him was a huge bag.

"Tomo! Mattie!" he shouted, and grabbed the raccoon. Hugging his pet, he asked Tomo, "Where have you been?"

"In the forest," Tomo said casually, "and beyond to my village."

"Then you *did* go to your village?" Nat said. "Where did you find Mattie?" There were so many questions Nat wanted answered.

"Indians had big harvest. White men didn't," Tomo said. "I went to my village to get maize so you would not starve this winter. You were sad because the provisions were low. I wanted to help you."

"Felix was certain you had a good reason for going," Nat said. "But why didn't you tell me?"

"If I could not get maize, story would not have right ending," the Indian boy explained. "Tomo didn't want good friend to be sad." Then his face brightened. "I have other bags by the big oak tree. Other Indians help carry them."

"You are my friend!" Nat was smiling. "Where did you find Mattie?"

"In the forest."

"I've searched every day for Mattie and you."

"Maybe Matoaka hid," Tomo said. "I saw raccoon and friend up in a tree. I called to her. She looked down. I saw her collar. I knew it was Matoaka."

"I'll never know the forest the way you do." Nat shook his head.

"You know many things I will never know." Tomo looked around the glass house. "You work here? Do you like it?"

"Yes," Nat said enthusiastically. He called to Felix.

"Welcome back," the glassblower said. "And you brought the raccoon. That is a double welcome!"

"We both wanted to come back to Jamestown," Tomo said, looking at the animal that had snuggled up in Nat's arm.

"When you were with the other Matoaka and your friends, didn't you want to stay with them?" Nat asked.

"Indians expect me to learn English," Tomo answered. "White boy is learning our language fast. We have big job to do."

"You surely have," Felix spoke up. "Do you think you want another job? We need you here to help Nat in the glass house."

"If work not in kitchen, maybe," Tomo answered.

"We'll talk about it another day," Felix said kindly. Then he turned to Nat. "Why don't Tomo and you take the raccoon back to her pen?"

"But I haven't finished my work yet," Nat said.

"The wanderers have returned. That calls for a celebration."

"It does!" Nat said as he started for the door, with Tomo following at his heels.

They put the raccoon in her pen and got fresh water and grass. Then they patched up the hole where she had slipped through.

"Please don't ever leave me again," Nat pleaded to Tomo. Then he remembered the bags of corn. "We left the maize at the glass house, and we have to get the other bags from the woods. How grateful the settlers will be to you!"

"They are my friends," the Indian boy said.

Nat couldn't wait until all the men who had accused Tomo of spying knew the truth about what he had done for the settlement.

13

Beads for Barter

GOVERNOR SMITH's large black hat didn't sit as jauntily as usual on his head when he and the four men marched into the fort upon their return from Chief Powhatan's village. Nat thought he saw defeat in his proud, stern face.

He had expected the governor to be jubilant, bursting with news about the elaborate plans for the chieftain's coronation. Instead, he even seemed reluctant to talk about it except to say that the ceremony would not be in Jamestown but at the chief's own village.

"So he has refused to come here?" Captain Newport frowned and his voice showed bewilderment. The men who had gathered around the two leaders shook their heads.

"Yes," Governor Smith nodded. "He doesn't trust us. He thinks it's safer to stay outside our fort."

"He's suspicious?" the captain asked. "This is a gesture of friendship!" He sounded impatient.

"Why shouldn't he be suspicious?" Governor Smith asked. "Have we ever paid him for the land we've settled?"

Captain Newport ignored that question.

"Chief Powhatan wields great power over those thirty or more Indian tribes," Governor Smith continued. "There are at least fifteen thousand Indians including fifteen hundred warriors in the Powhatan federation. That chieftain has pride, too, just like King James. Holding his head high and looking down at me, he said, 'If your king has sent me presents, I also am a king and this is my land. Your father is to come to me, not I to him.' "

"That settles it," Captain Newport said. "We will have to follow the chieftain's wishes. At this point I would be willing to drop the matter, but I can't. The London Company gave explicit orders that he was to be crowned." He paused. "We can't delay any longer. The Indians already may have a plan to attack us. We must flatter and pacify them—the sooner the better."

"What shall we do about the presents?" the governor asked.

"We shall send them around by water, and you and I with fifty soldiers will leave very soon by land."

Nat had looked forward to the ceremony at Jamestown. He and Tomo expected to be present. But now he would have to figure out a way to persuade Captain Newport and Governor Smith to let them attend the coronation at Werowocomoco.

Nat hurried to the glass house. He mustn't be late. He liked the work and hoped never to disappoint Felix. So far the glassblower seemed to be satisfied with him. Today Felix had told him he wouldn't have to work while Tomo was there. He hoped, as did Felix, that the Indian boy would decide that he wanted to work with glass.

Tomo was waiting at the door of the glass house as Nat came through the woods. When Nat told him about Chief Powhatan's answer to Governor Smith, he said, "That is right. He is proud like your king."

So Tomo agreed with the chief. That was natural.

They entered the glass house together. Nat blinked his eyes at the display of glass Felix and his helpers had arranged. It shimmered in the morning sun. Other times when Nat had looked at the bottles and vials, they had seemed dull and dark. But not today. The glass reflected all shades of green from light emerald to a deep forest green.

"You make all these?" Tomo asked, his eyes getting big like saucers. "What color are they?"

"Common green."

"Color like beautiful water in river where little fish play," Tomo said. "Wish other Indians could see green glass."

Nat had hoped Tomo would be interested in the glass articles, but he hadn't expected him to be so enthusiastic. Even when he was pleased, he generally didn't show it in this way.

If this color appealed to Tomo, why couldn't the glassblowers make something that the Indians would like to have? Nat thought. What, for instance? He looked around. Most of the bottles were large. The Indians wouldn't know how to use them.

Tomo picked up one of the smaller vials and looked at it carefully. Taking a deerskin thong from around his waist, he tied the leather strip to the vessel and hung it around his neck.

Indians liked to decorate and adorn themselves, Nat knew. At Chief Powhatan's coronation they would mark their faces with bright clay and wear porcupine quills, raccoon and deer teeth around their necks. Maybe the glassblowers could make bright beads! Beads would appeal to the Indians! Nat looked at the glass vial Tomo was wearing so proudly. The settlers desperately needed articles for barter.

If Felix and the other glassblowers could make beads, then he could string them. Green beads would make a special gift for the chieftain—something he had never had before.

Later when Felix asked Tomo whether he would like to work in the glass house, the boy looked around. Black smoke curled out of the holes in the furnaces and the air was filled with gray haze. Tomo shook his head. "No blue sky. Bad weather here all the time. Maybe I could carry sand from the river."

"That would help us," Felix assured him. "We use more sand than any other ingredient." Nat was sure Tomo didn't understand the word ingredient, but at this point it really didn't make too much difference. At least he had said he would help.

Nat looked at the man who was sitting in the wooden chair. Another worker with a hollow iron tube was rolling some melted glass on the polished flat stone in front of the furnace.

"What's he making?" Nat asked.

"Later on it will be a bottle," Felix said.

"Tomo, let's go over and watch," Nat suggested.

"No," the Indian boy answered. "I want to see Mattie."

"You can see her later," Nat reasoned.

"I want to shoot some game in the woods," Tomo said firmly.

It was useless to try to persuade him. Nat had found that he had a mind of his own, just like Chief Powhatan.

Nat watched Tomo as he left the glass house and disappeared into the forest.

"A pretty girl will cook my supper tonight," Nat said as he followed Felix over to the other side of the furnace.

The glassmaker turned around. "That means you will be at the Forrest home. Will John be there?"

"I think so."

They both smiled. They both knew how very interested John was in Ann Burras.

"Romance is exciting," Felix said changing the subject, "but you still have much to learn about glassmaking." Felix touched Nat's shoulder. "It looks like the melted glass is just the way we want it. We mixed the sand, potash, lime and ashes a couple days ago and then placed the mixture in the pots. The next day we added more frit and cullet until the pots were full. We mixed it well by stirring the stuff with this iron rake." Felix picked up a long tool with two prongs. "At first there is only a sticky mass in the pots," he went on, "but gradually the material liquifies and takes on the appearance of melted glass. The impurities that come to the surface look like white spongy scum. We call this *sand gall* or *sandever*. Of course we have to remove it."

"It must be lots of work," Nat said.

"But we've just begun the process of glassmaking," Felix laughed good-naturedly. "The next day we increased the heat in the furnace until we got a true glass. The fire was then slackened just enough so that this morning, when the crew came in, the melted mass was the right temperature."

"How do you know when it is ready?" Nat asked.

"We test the glass from time to time by dipping out a small amount and letting it string out into a thread." He turned and pointed. "See those testing threads around here?"

Nat saw the film of threads floating in the air like cobwebs.

"Now we're about ready for the first step to fashion a bottle. Watch the servitor. He is the one who helps the master."

Nat watched the servitor put his hollow iron into the pot containing the hot liquid and slowly turn the tool over and over. He took out a blob of glass, enough for the bottle he intended to make. The melted glass stuck to the iron like foam.

"That blob on the end of the blowing iron is called a 'gather,' " Felix said.

While the liquid was still red hot, the servitor rolled his hollow iron back and forth on the polished flat stone in front of one of the furnaces.

Nat was especially interested when the servitor gently blew into his hollow iron which seemed to inflate the melted glass just as blowing into a glove makes it swell. As often as he blew into the iron, which he seemed to do often, he removed the iron quickly from his mouth to his cheek.

"If he didn't do that," Felix explained, "the flame would go into his mouth when he blew into the iron again."

The servitor took his iron and whirled it gracefully many times about his head. He probably did it also to cool the glass, Nat thought, which got longer and longer.

While the servitor had been giving the glass its general shape, Felix explained that at this stage the glass is called the *paraison*. In the meantime the master workman had dipped his iron rod into the pot and had collected a small blob of glass that stuck to his tool.

"The master is using a *ponte,*" Felix said. "His tool is

also a solid iron rod, but it is shorter than the blowing iron that the other man is using. Because the *ponte* is larger at one end, the glass will stick to it better."

"You'll have to explain some of these tools and expressions to me again," Nat said, scratching his head. "I guess I know what the master and the servitor do, and I think I recognize a blowing iron and the *ponte*."

"That's one reason why you'll be an apprentice for several years," Felix smiled. "We know this is a special art and that only through constant practice does the glassblower at last perfect his work." Then he paused. "Glassmaking has a vocabulary all its own. But now I'm really going to bombard you with new words!"

Nat followed Felix as he walked closer to the master glassmaker. "With this second gather of melted glass, the *ponte* is now attached securely to the *paraison* or other hot glass. The master workman now presses the new gather against the end of the *paraison* exactly opposite the point where it is still attached to the blowing iron. The master workman then cracks or cuts the *paraison* from the blowing iron which the servitor is holding. By this time the glass has probably cooled too much to work, so the master workman holds it at the working hole of the furnace and brings it back to a workable temperature. He then goes to his chair where he keeps other tools he will now need." It looked to Nat like a crude wooden bench with flat arms extending out in front of the seat.

The master workman, now seated in the chair, rolled the *ponte* back and forth over the arms of the chair, at the same time widening and shaping the pliable glass. Nat could see that it was really shaping into something other than a long thick green thread. Several times the master reheated the glass.

Nat saw several tools hanging on wooden pegs at the

edge of the chair. They looked like scissors and clippers. The master workman probably used them to cut and shape the glass article.

"When it is finished, the glass is still very hot," Felix said, as Nat watched the master workman use the tools with sure motions. "Now the glass will have to cool gradually to give it the necessary final strength."

The workman suddenly gave the iron rod a sharp blow. The glass came off the *ponte.* Then one of the helpers carried it over with a forked stick to a smaller oven.

Felix went on. "Here at Jamestown we stack the glass objects at the back of the leer—that's the annealing oven. When that space is filled, then we block up the opening and let the fire go out. It's the gradual cooling of the hot stone oven that gives the desired annealing effect. We subject the glass first to very high heat, then we cool it to soften it thoroughly and to make it less brittle."

When Nat asked what annealing meant, Felix said: "It is the process of exposing the glass first to high heat, then letting it cool slowly so that it will not be so fragile or breakable. It really is a primitive way." Felix shook his head. "Someday I hope a glassmaker will invent a method that is more satisfactory."

"How long will that glass stay in the leer?" Nat asked. He used the new word proudly.

"In two or three days we'll open the oven. Then we will store the finished article in the bins along the south side of the glass house."

"Do you think I will ever be able to master all of it?" Nat asked. He had been fascinated by every step Felix had showed him. He was more aware than ever how cleverly the glassmakers used their tools. Nat also marveled that the master workman always seemed to know just when the melted glass was the right temperature to mold.

"Of course you will learn these skills," Felix assured him. "But it will take several years. When you become a master, you will be a proud artist."

Nat nodded slowly. He was already dreaming of that time.

"By the way," Felix said, changing the subject. "Will you give a message to Mistress Forrest when you go there tonight?"

"Surely, Felix," Nat said.

"Tell her that I hope to make window glass next week. If she would like to watch me, she can come next Wednesday afternoon. Also tell her that the panes will be diamond-shaped."

When Nat asked Felix about glass beads, he wasn't too encouraging. "They are difficult to make, and there are so many possible failures. But we'll try," he added. "It's time you reported to your other work. Good-by."

Later, when Nat hurried to his cabin, after having finished the kitchen chores for the day, he thought of the evening ahead of him. This was the first chance he had had to eat somewhere other than with the men. He wanted to visit with the two women, especially Ann.

Nat tried to shine his worn-out boots, but they didn't look much better after he had spent a long time cleaning them. He combed his hair carefully, grateful for the haircut Felix had given him.

Ann came to the door in response to his knock. "We're glad to see you," she said. Nat followed her into the large room where the Forrests and John were. Mistress Forrest suggested that he sit on the stool by the fireplace.

For dinner Ann served Yorkshire pudding with roasted venison and boiled corn. She had made the batter pudding and had baked it with the meat. John had shot the deer. Everything tasted good. Nat enjoyed drinking his tea from a delicate cup. The fine white china seemed like transparent silk.

After dinner, while they were grouped around the hearth listening to the logs crackle, Mistress Forrest turned to Nat. "My husband said that he understands the men in your cabin have violent arguments and fist fights," she said. "Would you like to live with us?" she asked gently. "We have an extra room we now use to store things, but if you wanted to come here to stay, we would get that room ready."

Nat was too surprised to speak. Something rose in his throat and choked him. These people wanted him! "I'd like to very much."

Nat thought of Tomo. If he came to live with the Forrests, would this mean he would see less of his friend? If he was to have a room to himself, maybe Tomo could share it.

"Could Tomo share that room with me?" he asked hesitantly.

Mrs. Forrest looked at her husband. "We hadn't thought of him. He is of a different race."

Nat wondered why that should matter. If she felt that way, it meant Tomo would not be welcome in her home. He thought a long while, then he said, "Thank you, Mistress Forrest, for your kind invitation, but Tomo and I are good friends and if I came to live here, he might be unhappy. Maybe he wouldn't want to see much of me any more."

"Tomo isn't as clean as you are," she said.

"Tomo swims in the river every morning, winter and summer," Nat said, defending his friend. "He takes baths more often than I do because I don't like the cold river water in the winter."

Soon he thanked his hosts, and John and Ann accompanied him to the door.

As he passed the row of houses he was regretful. It would have been much more pleasant living in a comfortable house with the Forrests instead of the dreary cabin full of disgruntled men. But the freedom to see his friend whenever he wanted to meant more to him.

14

Crown for Chief Powhatan

NAT COULDN'T MAKE Tomo enthusiastic about seeing the ceremony for Chief Powhatan.

"Wa-hun-son-a-cock doesn't want a crown," Tomo said. "He wants more feathers in his headdress. What does a crown mean to an Indian chief?"

"A crown is a royal headdress," Nat tried to explain. "But this one for Chief Powhatan is made of shining yellow gold instead of feathers. The crown is the greatest honor we can give him. Only the king in England has the right to wear a crown."

When Nat saw all the presents spread out, he wondered whether the coronation was as important as Captain Newport and the London Company considered it to be. The gifts had taken up much valuable space on the ship. He looked at the large bed with a fancy silk coverlet, the wide-mouthed jug, the expensive clothes and the other costly things. What would the chief ever do with a four-poster bed? Like Tomo, he probably preferred to sleep on fragrant pine boughs instead of on a mattress of old feathers or straw.

If the London Council had sent the right kind of cargo instead of filling the hold of the *Mary Margaret* with useless gifts, Jamestown would now be better off. And there were those cold winter months ahead with more settlers than ever to feed.

After many trials Felix and the other glassblowers had made a dozen green beads. Nat carefully put each bead on the leather thong and securely tied knots between them. Tomo liked the string of emerald beads. Nat knew the real test would come when Chief Powhatan received that gift. If he liked it, then beads should be good for barter.

"You should represent the workers of the glass house at the coronation," Felix suggested, "and present the beads to Chief Powhatan."

"That would be an honor, Felix," Nat said. "But I don't know whether the governor and the council will let me even go to the Indian village."

Several evenings later Governor Smith called Nat to his

lodgings. "How much of the Indian language do you know?" he asked.

"A little, Your Honor."

"How much?" the governor asked sharply, pulling on his heavy beard.

"Sir," Nat answered, "I know the Indian words for the birds, the animals, the flowers and trees in the forest, and I understand some of the sign language."

"Does Tomo know English well enough to serve as a translator for us?"

"I think so." Nat nodded. "He'll do the best he can."

"We'll use Thomas Savage also as an interpreter," Governor Smith said.

After several long sessions the council decided that Tomo and Nat should attend the coronation. They would be needed as interpreters. Because the two boys were good friends, the members agreed that Nat should go with the Indian boy. They felt Tomo would do a better job if Nat were there to help him.

A week later fifty men, led by Captain Newport and Governor Smith, marched proudly into Werowocomoco. Tomo and Nat followed close behind. The men's silk and velvet doublets and breeches were as brilliant as the feathers of the scarlet tanager and bluebird. The plumes on the wide hats bobbed wildly. Nat felt equally proud. He was wearing for the first time new boots with wide bands and metal buckles that Felix had given him. Of those who traveled from Jamestown, Tomo wore the least clothes.

Nat looked forward to meeting Chief Powhatan, whose father had also been a great chief. His empire included at least thirty Indian tribes. Nat hadn't expected him to be so tall, because most of the Indians he had seen were of medium height. But the chieftain had a sour look.

Perhaps he was suspicious of the white men assembled in his village. Chief Powhatan's hair was like pepper and salt and he had hardly any beard. Nat looked at the Englishmen. Everyone had a beard, some longer than others. Many of the Indians had shaved their heads while the black hair of the others glistened.

Spread out in the clearing were the costly gifts from the English. Nat thought the carved mahogany bed was wholly out of place.

With pomp and ceremony the two captains placed the scarlet cloak on Chief Powhatan's shoulders, while others spread out the train. But when Captain Newport and Governor Smith tried to get the chieftain to kneel to receive the crown, he raised his head proudly. One of the Englishmen tried to show by example what they wanted him to do, but he continued to stand up haughtily, shaking his head.

In desperation Captain Newport beckoned to Tomo and Thomas Savage. First Thomas and then Tomo spoke to Chief Powhatan in his native tongue. He said a few words to them which Nat did not understand.

At last by forcing his shoulders down, they made him stoop a little. Then they quickly pressed the crown on his head.

At that moment a musket shot rang through the air, followed by loud reports from other guns. Chief Powhatan was completely unnerved. His eyes filled with sudden fear as he hugged the cloak closer to him. He muttered something to Thomas and Tomo.

The Indian boy turned to Captain Newport and translated what the chieftain had said, "Is this a plan to slaughter me and my people?"

"Explain to your chief," Captain Newport said hastily to Tomo, "that we do not intend to harm him or his people. The guns are a king's salute. They are honoring him. We are his friends."

Tomo then translated the captain's message into his native tongue. Chief Powhatan nodded with relief.

Nat had looked forward to presenting the beads to the chieftain. He hadn't expected Chief Powhatan to be so terrified by the musket shots. Bewildered, Nat held the beads tightly in his hands. He didn't know what to do. Perhaps Powhatan wouldn't like this gift. Yet when he had showed the beads to the chief's daughter, she had been happy about them and had begged for them herself.

Now she poked Nat. "The beads," Matoaka said, motioning with a slim brown hand.

Slowly Nat walked over to the chieftain and held out the beads. His arm was shaking. "For you, from Tomo and me."

Chief Powhatan looked at Nat. He smiled and reached out his hand for the beads. As he placed them around his neck over the heavy silk and velvet robe, the glass sparkled.

The beads had passed the test!

"When will you make some beads for me?" Matoaka whispered.

"After the big ship sails back to England," Nat promised her.

15

Glass, Frankincense and Clapboard

WHEN CAPTAIN NEWPORT and the venturers left on the gold-hunting expedition shortly after the coronation, Nat found that he wasn't envious of them. He hoped very much they would find the gold. Then the colonists and the London Company would be satisfied. He hated the constant pressure from the company that had started Jamestown. Everything seemed to be done in terms of money. The interests of the settlers didn't seem to matter.

Felix reported to Nat the decision about the glass beads. "I talked to Captain Newport before he left," he said. "As many glass articles as possible must be made and packed in the *Mary Margaret* by the time he returns. But that doesn't include beads."

"We have to have food to exist and the Indians will only trade maize if they like the things we offer them. Matoaka told me she'd trade popcorn for bead necklaces."

"What's popcorn?" Felix asked.

"Popcorn is the best food in the world!" Nat said enthusiastically. "Of course, you haven't eaten it yet. We've never raised any here, but maybe we will next year, if I can get some seed from Pocahontas." Nat's mouth watered. "The grains really pop! You put the rounded kernels in an iron pan over a blazing fire. You keep shaking or moving the kettle. The grains enlarge six or eight times and then explode. Then you have light, delicious kernels that look more like clusters of white blossoms, except that they are good to eat. Add some salt and you have a dish fit for a king."

"Sounds good to eat," Felix said. "But if the popcorn depends on the glass beads, we'll have to wait awhile. Right now I'm depending on you to help pack the fragile glass."

Nat's period of apprenticeship was being delayed these days. He spent his time packing glass articles with straw and then carefully placing them in wooden boxes.

Nat caressed every vial and bottle that he packed. He considered each one a work of art, and he appreciated them all the more because now he knew how difficult they were to make and how easy it was to have a failure. As soon as the boxes were filled, men transported them to the ship.

"We didn't have any bottles in our home in London," Nat said. "What will they use them for?"

"The apothecaries keep medicine in the big bottles and the vials will be used to hold perfume," Felix explained. "Some people in the shops and homes now use large glass bottles to store all kinds of liquids instead of using earthernware." Felix had not stopped his work as he talked. "There's a big demand for glass in England these days!"

Although Nat had no regrets about not going on the expedition, he was impatient to have the men back again with good news.

All the colonists including Mistress Forrest, Ann Burras, Nat and Felix, were at the main gate when the men returned.

"Where's the gold?" someone called out.

"Did you find the Lost Colony?" another asked.

"What about a way to the western sea?"

The venturers hung their heads as they looked at Captain Newport. "Not gold but silver!" He held up a lump of ore.

What a disappointment! Nat knew that silver did not have the value that gold had. How would the London Company receive this news? Would some of the adventurers now return to England on the *Mary Margaret?* They might, since they hadn't found gold in Virginia. If they stayed, they would have to work in the glass house or fell trees or prepare the fields for crops.

Captain Newport turned to Governor Smith. "With this poor trial I am contented to leave this fair, fertile, well-watered country."

"What about the food supplies from the Indians you promised to get while you were away?" Governor Smith asked him directly.

"Every day the Indians are getting more independent," Captain Newport said. "Jamestown may be in danger."

"We'll meet that problem when they attack us," Governor Smith answered casually. At least he was not afraid. It was good that a man of his strength and confidence was the president. "Now that you have come back, I'll leave immediately with thirty men. We'll go down the river to fell trees and make clapboard. We intend also to collect frankincense. The resin is a good remedy for many diseases."

The next day the Polish and German glassmakers returned to work at the factory. Governor Smith ordered Nat to chop trees. Did this mean he wouldn't be Felix's apprentice? When he asked the glassmaker, Felix tried to explain that the colony was in a state of emergency, that life would surely calm down after the supplies were in the ship. Nat wasn't so sure, but he didn't dare disobey Governor Smith's order.

Nat found using an ax was hard work. From sunrise to sunset he swung the ax, chopping down trees. His hands and those of the others were blistered. As they looked at their sore hands, the men around him cursed violently.

When the governor heard them he was furious and his face burned with rage. He turned to one of the soldiers in charge. "Take this order. A can of water shall be poured down a man's sleeve for each oath."

"We all swear under our breath," one of the men said, rubbing his hands.

"God interferes directly in the affairs of men," Governor Smith said, raising himself to his full height. "Any act which causes His displeasure has direct consequences. No one shall be allowed to swear so long as I am governor."

Nat had not known that Governor Smith felt this strongly about swearing.

"As leader of Jamestown," Governor Smith went on, "it is my duty to see that God has no excuse for punishing this colony."

The men were impressed by his sincerity and respect for God. It seemed to Nat that they now worked harder than ever, even though their hands were raw and tender.

"We've scarcely heard an oath this week," the governor said to Captain Newport, as Nat stood near them. "But felling trees and making clapboards and wainscot, and collecting the gum resin," he added, "are not as important to the survival of the colony as food is. You will leave shortly for England, but I remain and I am responsible to my people. I am taking a barge up the Chickahominy River soon to see if I can get food where you have failed." He turned to Nat. "I intend to take some beads with me," he said kindly.

16

Fire in the Forest

WHILE GOVERNOR SMITH bartered with the Indians for maize, Captain Newport let Nat return to the glass house as an apprentice. He was more contented than he had been for a long time. As he dreamed of the day when he would make graceful bottles from colored glass, Nat hummed a merry tune.

The fires in the furnace burned furiously. Nat reheated some of the hot liquid. He was pleased that he had already learned so much about glassmaking.

Since a great deal of smoke was always coming from the furnaces, Nat had grown accustomed to the smell and the gray haze. He was not aware that there was any more smoke in the glass house than usual.

All at once his musings were interrupted by a frantic call from the forest. "Fire! Fire!" It was Tomo. The Indian boy ran into the glass house and over to Nat. "Come!"

"Fire?" Nat exclaimed. "Where?" His fear of fire swept over him. He stood rooted in front of the main furnace. Could he ever live through another fire?

"In the woods, all around the glass house. Come!"

Nat looked outside. The evergreen trees in front of the building were in flames. He shouted to Felix and the other men and they all started running. They stopped when they saw the blazing forest in front of them.

"We are trapped!" one of the men screamed.

"We are trapped!" the rest echoed.

Nat saw they were doomed.

Trees crackled and crashed to the ground. The fire burned fiercely.

Tomo called out to the men, "Follow me." His voice was so calm that Nat wondered if he had ever been in a forest fire before.

Pulling at Nat's shirt, Tomo tore it off, and, turning back into the glass house, he plunged it into a tub of water. With quick motions he ripped it into smaller pieces and gave wet cloths to each man.

"Cover your faces! Follow me!" The Indian boy commanded. In single file he led them out of the glass house.

"Which way do we go?" Nat shrilled. His nostrils and eyes smarted from the heavy smoke. Where could Tomo lead them? But he was their only hope!

The Indian boy hesitated for a moment, then dropped

quickly to the ground, motioning for the others to do the same. They crawled slowly on their hands and knees through prickly underbrush. Nat saw a fox dash through the black smoke.

Would they ever get out of this fire trap? Nat realized that he mustn't be afraid. All at once he felt a new kind of courage, something he had never experienced before. A burning tree crashed in front of him. He got up quickly and jumped over it. The men behind him did the same.

After a long time of crawling and choking through the brush, Tomo led them out into a clearing. They were safe now! Nat saw John waiting for them. He and others had hurried from the fort.

"How do you think the fire started?" Nat asked John, after he had had a chance to breathe some fresh air.

"The wind must have carried hot cinders from the furnaces to the grass and leaves around the glass house," John said. "It hasn't rained for a long time and the woods are unusually dry."

"We were so busy working inside we didn't know the trees and bushes were on fire."

"But fortunately Tomo did," John said with a shudder. "There's still a brisk breeze. The glass house is hopeless, but we can't let the fort burn!"

John and the other men ran toward the settlement.

Nat and Tomo hurried to rescue Mattie. As Nat quickly picked her up, she nestled in his arms. "What shall we do with her?" he asked.

"We will tie Mattie to a tree near the river bank," Tomo said. "She will be safe by the water."

Men lugging buckets and pots and pans raced to the James River to get water and then headed toward the fort.

Captain Newport was working tirelessly along with the others. "I wish Governor Smith were here," he said as he stopped for a moment to wipe ashes from his face and beard. "He would know what to do!"

This was the first time Nat was aware that Captain Newport depended on the governor! "He always knows what to do," Nat said aloud.

Felix and John organized the settlers who fought the fire. Tomo and Nat helped hand buckets to men, who filled them with water, while some dozen more raced with the buckets to the edge of the fire. Still others tried to stamp out the angry flames with brooms and their heavy boots.

"We can't let the fire get any closer to the fort," John called frantically to Nat. "We must make a clearing wide enough so that the flames can't possibly go beyond that point!"

Tomo and Nat began pulling at the dried bushes and small trees, clearing a wide space. The wind, that only a short while before was blowing hard, gradually stopped.

"Our Heavenly Father is watching over us," Nat said reverently.

For hours they fought the fire until finally they had it under control.

"At least the fort is saved," Nat sighed, looking at Tomo and Felix. "We won't let the glass house stay in ruins, will we? Can't we start building it again very soon?" he asked hopefully.

"The council has to decide," Felix said. "But I hope we can rebuild at once."

John had just joined them. "I am ready to start tomorrow!" he said.

Neither Felix or John would admit defeat. Vicar Hunt's words rang again in Nat's ears: "You are bigger than anything that can ever happen to you!" John and

Felix wouldn't let a fire destroy them. They had courage. And Nat wasn't going to let a fire destroy him either!

A few days later Governor Smith returned to Jamestown. He had succeeded in getting a supply of maize from the Indians. Nat heard him tell John that he hoped soon to leave on a more extensive trip inland for the same purpose, but he would wait until the glassmakers could rebuild their house and could make some more beads for barter. He praised the men for their good work in saving the fort. He had a special word of praise for Nat, and for Tomo's presence of mind.

The hold of the *Mary Margaret* was now loaded with glass, pitch tar, frankincense, soap ashes, clapboard and wainscoting. Any day Captain Newport would sail to England.

One fine morning the sails went up and the *Mary Margaret* headed eastward for the Atlantic Ocean. Nat wasn't as excited about the ship now as he had been when it arrived a few months before. He looked at Tomo who was watching it with great interest.

"That's a big ship," Tomo said.

"Would you like to be sailing to England?" Nat asked.

"No." Tomo shook his head. "Would you?"

"My home is Jamestown, and my country is Virginia," Nat answered. "My friends and Mattie are here."

"This is a good place," Tomo nodded.

"I'll tell you a secret, Tomo," Nat whispered in his ear. "I want to give one of Mattie's babies as a wedding gift to Ann and John when they get married."

"What is married?" Tomo asked. This was a new word to him. The wedding would be the first in Jamestown.

Nat tried to explain to Tomo what marriage was. "Someday I will marry and have my own home here," Nat told him. Tomo looked puzzled, so Nat changed the subject. "I have good news. John is building a large cabin and he has room for us. We will be living with John and Ann. We can even have Mattie's pen close by!"

Tomo nodded and smiled. He liked the idea.

Nat looked toward the woods. They had already started to rebuild the glass house. The stone furnaces had not suffered from the fire and fortunately they had found most of the tools undamaged. He dreamed once again of the time when he would be making glass.

"Let's go to the glass house, Tomo," Nat said. "We can help the men. At least we can gather the reeds for the thatched roof. The sooner the glass house is ready, the sooner I'll be a master glassblower."

The two boys turned from the river and started toward the glass house. Together they would be a part of the new house that would rise from the ashes of the old, a part of the new country that would blend the Old World with the New.

and her sister Virginia were the first twins born in the town of Riverton, Wyoming, that bordered on the Wind River Indian Reservation. The girls' parents had gone there, after finishing college in Iowa and Nebraska, to homestead on prairie land opened up by the Government. Their father later became Judge Dobler. To get to the new town, the Doblers had to travel by a stagecoach as well as train. The kindly Episcopal clergyman from the British Isles, who was spiritual guide to the Indians, baptized the Dobler twins.

Later, the family moved to the West Coast, where the twins were graduated from the University of California, at Berkeley. Then the girls' paths separated, and Lavinia went to Puerto Rico, to teach English and become an English supervisor. For the past twelve years Miss Dobler has been librarian at Scholastic Magazines, Inc., New York City, where she works on the historical and contemporary material published in the many Scholastic magazines for boys and girls.

Indians were a definite part of Miss Dobler's childhood. At the annual celebrations held in Riverton, the Arapahoes and Shoshones set up their tepees in the lowland near her home, and she learned the Indian dances directly from the bronze-skinned boys and girls. As early as the fifth grade, in Wyoming, Miss Dobler became deeply interested in American history. One subject of her research was Timothy Matlack, fighting Quaker, who was the penman for the Declaration of Independence. Several of her historical articles and stories were published previous to the appearance of her first book, *Glass House at Jamestown*. She made a special trip to Virginia while doing her research for this historical account of one of the youngest members of the famous Virginia colony and the first glass factory in America.